chest of secrets

Sweetfern Harbor Mystery - 10

wendy meadows

chapter one

The warm, late spring air matched Brenda's feeling of well-being. She and Mac sat outside in the backyard of Sheffield Bed and Breakfast and enjoyed the quiet sounds of the Atlantic Ocean lapping against the rocky shore nearby. The framing for their new home, nearly completed, seated just over the lawn, gave pleasure to both. Brenda referred to it as their cottage, but as plans were solidified, both knew the end product promised to be a spacious structure, larger than the concept of a cottage.

"It will be great to finally move into our own place, Mac. I've loved the apartment in the bed and breakfast but we need this."

Mac shifted so his arm reached around his wife's shoulder. "I'm looking forward to that, too, Brenda." He paused as if formulating his words. "Do you think we're going too big with it?"

"We have to look far ahead. If our bed and breakfast continues to be successful, this new structure could become a future annex. We're turning guests away now because of lack of space."

Mac chuckled softly. "I do hope that's in the faraway future. As for me, I want to live there with you for the rest of our lives."

They talked of the architecture Brenda had discussed with the architect, Rich Turner. Brenda was adamant it should match the 1890 Queen Anne mansion bed and breakfast she inherited from her uncle, Randolph Sheffield. She watched every detail as Rich and his crew stripped down the old summer house and gradually, the home of their dreams began to emerge.

Mac's cell phone rang and he gave Brenda a regretful look. Detective Mac Rivers rarely managed to catch moments totally alone with Brenda, but she understood that his job was a demanding one.

After a short conversation, Mac nodded. "This can wait until morning, Bryce. Let's let him think about it for a while. Go ahead and book the man and I'll be there bright and early."

Mac explained to Brenda that their son-in-law, Detective Bryce Jones, had successfully nabbed the man believed to be responsible for recent break-ins around Sweetfern Harbor. Until it became a tourist attraction, the small village experienced very little crime. Mac didn't want to mar the tranquility of the night. They sat in silence and listened to the ocean sounds and thinking happily about the future.

The next morning, Allie Williams arrived on time as usual. The young reservationist loved her job at the historic bed and breakfast. She dealt well with all guests and lived a full life at age seventeen. She planned to start college in the fall. Brenda hoped she would stay on at the bed and breakfast while she continued her schooling. The demand for Allie's unique and sometimes quirky paintings grew all the time, since she had the benefit of a little exposure whenever Brenda displayed them in the rooms of the house.

When Brenda came downstairs, she found Allie bent over the computer screen.

"It looks like we have a pretty good mix of guests arriving for the weekend, Brenda." She pointed out the towns and cities the guests came from. "I hope they get along well."

"They will. You are really great at helping that along when we have guests who take longer than others to join in."

Brenda proceeded to the dining room where she and her head housekeeper, Phyllis Pendleton, met routinely before starting their day. They were alone, since the previous night's guests had checked out and new ones had not yet arrived. Phyllis asked Brenda about the progress of their new home. That question was all it took for Brenda to delve into the subject with enthusiasm. Allie joined them and poured a cup of hot chocolate for herself. After a while, she started to go back to the front desk.

"Wouldn't it be something if they dug up a buried treasure out there?"

Young Allie and sixty-year old Phyllis were equals when it came to their imaginations running wild. "It's very possible that something is buried out there. This place has been around a long time," Phyllis said. "Maybe you should tell Rich and his men to dig carefully. We have no idea what secrets are hidden in this place."

Brenda didn't have time to answer.

"What if dead bodies are buried out there?" Allie said.

Brenda held up her hand to stop both of them. "No dead bodies are buried in the yard, don't be silly," she said, though privately she thought the possibility of hidden treasure wasn't unreasonable. "Maybe they'll find a few dropped pennies or something." She shook her head, realizing she was as bad as the other two when it came to an overactive imagination. "Do you two remember the silver skeleton key I found in the attic when I first took over the B&B? The one that didn't fit any locks in the house?" Both Allie and Phyllis nodded.

Phyllis asked, "Did you ever find out what that key was for, Brenda?"

"I'm sure it's probably for one of Randolph's old trunks or jewelry boxes. It's in very good condition and I brought it down to our apartment. I've never found that it fits any locks in the bed and breakfast. But there are nooks and crannies I am still finding. Maybe the builders will dig up an old lock that will fit the key?"

Allie took her hot chocolate and told them she was going to work on sketches for her next drawings until the guests started arriving. Phyllis and Brenda finished their beverages. They took a walk through the guest rooms to make sure everything was in order. When they came back downstairs, Brenda's father, Tim Sheffield, came through the front entrance. The surprised look on Brenda's face caused her father to laugh.

"I'm surprised you didn't sneak in the back door," she

teased him. "Morgan is in the kitchen with some fresh cinnamon rolls."

Tim's smile spread wider. "Can't I say hello to my daughter first?" He leaned down and kissed Brenda on the forehead. Tim started down the hallway to the kitchen.

"When are you going to put a ring on Morgan's finger, Dad?" Brenda loved to tease her old-fashioned father. Everyone knew that he and the chef had become an item. Brenda had long been planning a party to celebrate their engagement, in case he ever made his move.

"We are getting to know one another," Tim said. He waved at them over his shoulder and picked up his pace.

It was two in the afternoon when the first guest finally arrived that day. Annette Pickard came in with an overnight bag, pulling a wheeled her suitcase behind her. She appeared to be in her early thirties and was very attractive. Dressed casually, she walked in with ease and a certain grace. Allie greeted her with her usual bubbly welcome. The guest appeared to cringe but managed a weak smile. Allie called the porter, Michael, to help with the bags while she checked her in.

"I also have my laptop and briefcase in the car," Annette said. Allie offered to get it for her but Annette turned to go back out, ignoring the offer. When she returned, her manner remained serious.

"I hope you enjoy your time here, Miss Pickard. Let us know if you need anything at all."

"I won't need anything and I prefer to be left alone. I'm a writer and I'm here for peace and quiet in order to finish a novel."

Allie didn't miss the fact that the guest wanted to be

left alone, but her curiosity overcame her. A real novelist was visiting! "What is your book about?" They were on the stairs by now.

"It's a story about a crime. It's fiction, though parts of it, I believe, are non-fiction."

Her serious demeanor prevented Allie from asking any more questions. She hoped that Annette Pickard would open up more during her stay. Allie's curiosity wasn't easily contained. She asked the guest if the room was satisfactory, lingering in the doorway for a moment. Annette looked out the back window that overlooked the yard and then walked to the side window. She seemed happy to notice she had a corner room with two views, but then she frowned.

"I hope whatever construction is going on out there won't disturb me with too much noise." Allie assured her the bed and breakfast was well insulated, and very little noise permeated. "I'll give it a try then."

Annette stared at Allie and the hint for the young girl to leave was obvious. She went back downstairs and heard Brenda and Phyllis discussing the weekend activities in Sweetfern Harbor. She knocked lightly on the opened door and walked in, describing their first guest.

"Please make sure no one disturbs her. She's not a very friendly person."

"We'll respect her wishes, Allie," Brenda said, "and make sure she has the privacy she prefers. Did you tell her the signal for dinnertime?" Allie said yes and then turned when she heard voices from the foyer.

Allie caught her breath when she saw the stylish couple approach her. Both were impeccably dressed in upscale attire, yet appeared casual enough to fit in among the population of Sweetfern Harbor and Sheffield Bed and Breakfast.

"Your jacket is beautiful," Allie said to the woman, Jane Clark, as she checked them in.

The fortyish Jane smiled and told her she had designed it herself. "I'm a designer of housewares in New York City, but dabble in clothing design as well. I'm lucky to have a husband who is a textile broker and can get his hands on excellent fabrics."

Logan Clark stepped forward and introduced himself. He was less talkative than his wife. Both had naturally sophisticated but warm manners. The porter appeared from the alcove and picked up their bags. Allie gave him their room number and the couple followed him upstairs. Logan Clark carried two more bags.

Michael showed them to the room next to Annette Pickard's. The spacious window brought in natural light and faced the side yard. Michael pointed out that the ocean was below the seawall. The waters in the distance were visible. He told them there was a pathway down to the beach area. He cautioned them to wear durable sandals or other shoes since they first had to walk over small rocks to get there.

"I'm looking forward to soaking up some sun," Jane said. Logan thanked Michael and slipped him a generous tip. As the porter left, he heard Jane saying, "Maybe this is a good choice after all, Logan. I had my doubts when you mentioned staying in this small seaside town."

Phyllis went into the room off the gathering room. She checked that all office supplies were available as well as the copier with paper. Jane and Logan Clark both requested ahead of time to have access to a business center in order to check in on their work. The guest office area was reserved for their use alone. She met the couple when they came back downstairs.

"I'll show you the office we provided for you." She led them to the room and handed them the key that opened the door. "Nothing will be disturbed and you are the only ones with access to the office, except for Brenda and me. We won't go in unless you ask for supplies that I may have overlooked."

Brenda heard the voices and came over to introduce herself. She welcomed the couple and told them that dinner would be served at seven that evening. Brenda pointed out the corner of the office where a coffee pot and basket of snacks were set. Tea bags were in a smaller basket nearby. She didn't repeat anything else regarding amenities, since Allie's job was to give that information when guests checked in. Refreshments and light snacks were available round the clock to all guests in the common area. Phyllis and Brenda left the couple after confirming that they had everything they needed.

They came into the front desk area just as two more young couples walked in. The two men talked about water sports. One of the women introduced them all. Lauren and Josh Meyers had been friends with Holly and Clint Evans since childhood. Josh and Clint never seemed to get enough of fun in the water, according to Holly, which was partly why they had chosen to visit Sweetfern Harbor.

Brenda was glad to greet guests who were so full of

life. All were in their early twenties. Fit bodies indicated exercise provided their main source of fun.

Brenda introduced herself and Phyllis. "There is someone in town that can be a resource for you if you want to learn new water sports," Brenda said. "Jonathan Wright owns a boat rental business near the harbor and he also teaches water sports."

"We're all for learning anything new that has to do with getting in the water. We grew up swimming in lakes and rivers mainly, so the ocean will be a new challenge for us," Josh said. All four agreed enthusiastically.

They insisted on carrying their own bags and Michael accompanied them to their rooms opposite the Clarks. Both couples were pleased with the rooms and Michael told them dinner would be served at seven. He left them to their chatter.

Meanwhile, downstairs, Brenda breathed a sigh of relief. She was thankful the two young couples brought life into the bed and breakfast, which should counteract the distant manner of Annette Pickard and the somewhat reserved Clarks.

chapter two

It had become a habit with Brenda and Mac to sit outside in the evenings and admire the progress of their new home. Brenda commented on the guests who had arrived so far.

"It seems like all eight rooms are booked again, Brenda."

"I think they are enjoying first impressions. Annette is holed up in her room, though. It's too bad she isn't giving herself time to enjoy the shops downtown."

"I suppose writers are like that. She did ask for peace and quiet."

"I may ask her if she would like a break tomorrow after breakfast. Phyllis and I plan to go down to Morning Sun Coffee. Molly is getting closer to Jon Wright and I think Phyllis worries about her daughter."

"The two of you shouldn't meddle. Molly is a grown woman now. The fact that she successfully runs and owns her own coffee shop should tell both of you something."

"If you recall," Brenda said, "Molly originally thought

she found the right person with the mailman, Pete Graham. We all know how that turned out." Pete Graham had been arrested in the end, as everyone in Sweetfern Harbor knew very well.

Mac gave up. He had learned early on that when Brenda and Phyllis set their minds on something it was hard to get them to budge. He stood up and stretched. "Come with me. I need a walk."

Brenda joined him and they walked toward the skeleton frame of their new home. Their builder Rich was taking advantage of the good weather and one wall was already in place. They noted where pipes would be laid. Brenda told Mac that she and Rich were set to meet in regard to the next steps the following morning. She hoped Mac could join them, but he told her he was swamped at work.

"You can call me if you have any questions when you meet with him, Brenda, but I just can't get away right now."

"I understand. Don't worry about it. We can count on Rich Turner doing a good job."

The next morning at ten, Rich left his crew to carry on and walked over to meet Brenda, who carried two tall glasses of iced tea. They sat at the round patio table and Rich began discussing the progress.

"It's all going quite well, Brenda. I called William Pendleton and he agreed to come over and give me a little more history of the architecture we're going for. William's knowledge is invaluable."

William Pendleton had lived in the area most of his life. Married to Phyllis, he was very involved in preserving history in the town. Brenda's and Mac's new home was no exception and he was happy to be consulted. The new home would look as if it had been built in the Queen Anne era, just like the bed and breakfast.

"I do have a question," Rich said. "We were digging a trench to place pipes in the kitchen area and we've hit something hard. Around here it could be sheer rock, but I want to tread carefully. William said we could easily find old abandoned foundations under the soil, or even relics that may be significant. I don't doubt it since the grounds have been occupied for such a long, long time."

"Maybe you will dig up buried treasure after all," Brenda said. When Rich's eyes became question marks, Brenda explained the silly notions Allie and Phyllis had about finding buried treasure. "As long as you aren't hitting a coffin or a gas line, I'm fine with treading carefully until you know what it is." She had to explain again. Both laughed.

He reassured her there were no buried gas lines in the area. "And I doubt it is a coffin, but something hard is there. I'll bring a bigger piece of machinery tomorrow. We'll be careful, but I think it's probably just rock." He sipped the cold drink. "I'm an avid reader of biographies of historic characters. I'm sure there are plenty of books out there that tell stories of this property before your uncle bought it."

"Hey, boss," a man's voice interrupted. "What do you want to do about that area where the kitchen pipes will go?" Rich snorted softly. "Do you think I can find anything interesting down there to add to my collection?" The younger man seemed to be half-joking but he did look intrigued by the idea.

"I told you to wait until tomorrow when I can get the other backhoe in here. As for anything interesting, whatever is found will go to the property owner, this woman right here."

He pointed to Brenda. Brenda had noticed Rich didn't have as much patience with the thirty-five year old Andy Shelton as he did with the others. Andy often helped build floats for parades during special Sweetfern Harbor events. Brenda liked his enthusiasm but there was clearly a thorn between the two men.

Rich thanked Brenda for the cold drink and discussion. He joined his workers and another wall went up before the day ended.

Sometime later that day, while Brenda was checking the blooming roses, William Pendleton walked around to the backyard. Everett Bennett, a well-known retired archaeologist in the area, accompanied him. He and William had reconnected years before after knowing each other in college. Brenda greeted them and called to Rich. She then left them to discuss matters of history and architecture. She was behind on her accounting in the office and knew that William would fill her in on the conversation later.

That evening, Brenda and Mac joined their guests at dinner. Holly Evans sat next to the novelist Annette and more than once attempted to draw her into the ongoing conversations. Holly was persistent and when she asked Annette her occupation, Annette answered.

"I'm a writer," she said. "I'm here to finish a novel that

my agent is waiting for. I'm afraid I'm woefully slow with it."

Holly was a casual reader and pleased to hear she had drawn this information out of the reluctant conversationalist. She felt successful to have gotten this far.

"What is the novel about?" Lauren asked. When Annette told her it was a mystery, Lauren became enthused. "I love to read mysteries. I will have to look for it when you are finished."

Annette seemed drawn out of her usual reserve. "I've written two before this one and both are available online. I write fiction, but can't help inserting things I believe may be true."

Logan Clark sat on the other side of Annette. "What is your last name so we can look you up?"

"It is Pickard." Annette pulled back, conscious of how much she had said. She felt Logan staring at her before he turned back to the last bite of salmon on his plate.

After everyone finished the main meal, Brenda invited them to the sitting room to have desserts. A variety of cakes and pies were readied on small dessert plates. Each guest chose one and carried the treats to the sitting room. Annette declined dessert but joined them with an after-dinner drink. Brenda and Mac socialized with them all and conversations flowed well.

Several times Annette felt Logan Clark's eyes on her. His eyes shifted away when she turned to him. Annette was happy to get back to her room as soon as she finished the last few sips of her drink. Something about the man caused uneasiness in her.

Brenda and Mac left their guests and took a walk around the perimeter of their new home. The full moon shone through the open wall that would soon enclose the kitchen. The backhoe Rich promised would arrive early the next morning. Mac picked up a stick beneath the nearby tree and began prodding in the spot where Brenda said Rich had felt something hard.

"Are you hoping to find that buried treasure, Mac?" Her teasing eyes caused something to stir within him. Brenda knelt down and brushed dirt away with her hands, curious herself.

"Look at that," Mac said. "Something is sticking out of the ground." He moved the stick back and forth. Brenda peered closer and then brushed more dirt away with her hands.

"I think it is just a metal sheet," she said. "Let me have the stick."

Mac handed it to her and Brenda started digging around the sheet of metal. Mac took it from her and dug as much as he could with the stick, which soon snapped in two. Both knelt down and gingerly began pushing loose dirt from around the object. It was soon discovered that whatever it was went deeper than a piece of flat tin.

"Be careful, Brenda, there may be sharp edges. I'll get a shovel." Mac went to the tool shed and came back with a hoe and a shovel. Together they continued to dig around the mystery item. When Mac took a breath from his exertions and shone his pocket flashlight down into the hole, he got more excited. "I see a box of some kind," Mac said.

Excitement surged through both of them. With Mac

prodding it with the shovel and Brenda on the other side of it with the garden hoe, they prized it out of the damp, thick soil. The metal chest was small but very heavy. Rust covered the bottom of it. Brenda was dismayed when she saw the locked padlock on the box.

"Can we clean the keyhole?" she asked Mac. She did not want to break it open, old as it was.

He rubbed his fingers over the hole. Some of the dirt loosened. "How do you expect to unlock it?"

Brenda snapped her fingers. "Maybe, just maybe, I have the answer. Wait right here and don't you dare crack it open before I get back, Mac Rivers." She jumped up and hurried to the apartment she and Mac shared. On her way back downstairs, Brenda stopped in the kitchen and opened the catch-all drawer. Taking the small can of WD-40 from it she hurried back outside. Mac continued to try to remove as much dirt as possible. "I have a possible answer," Brenda said. She waved the key in one hand and the WD-40 in the other. A rag hung over her left wrist.

Mac sprayed the formula and wiped it clean. Brenda handed him the silver skeleton key. "Oh, no. You do the honors, Brenda."

Her hands trembled slightly as she tried the key, which went right in. "Put your hand over mine, Mac. We'll turn it together." He happily obliged her. The lock protested sharply as it turned, then they heard the interior mechanism come undone.

Mac then lifted the lid. The two back hinges scraped and slowly the contents became visible. Inside was a large parchment envelope. The envelope bulged in places.

"Let's take it all upstairs to the apartment," Brenda

said. "We'll go up the back stairs to avoid waking up anyone." Mac agreed and she placed the parchment back where it had been. Her heart beat rapidly. "What do you think is in there?"

Mac laughed. "I have no idea, but I can tell you this is not a lightweight box. Let's go."

In the shadows, a figure lurked, watching the entire scene from beginning to end. There was nothing that could be done at this point. In time, things would return to the way they were before arriving at Sheffield Bed and Breakfast.

They managed to sneak up to their apartment without being seen. Brenda wanted the mysterious discovery all to herself and did not relish the idea of her staff or her guests getting too nosy before she figured out what it was. If it was a family secret, it might very well be something worth keeping in the shadows, she thought to herself.

Brenda spread out a newspaper on the dinette table and Mac placed the chest there. Under the ceiling light the chest looked old but not ancient. Mac determined it probably had been in the ground for perhaps thirty to fifty years at most, though neither could be sure. Brenda picked up the envelope again after they checked for other items inside. Mac sat down next to her. She set a worn leather bag on the table first. The strap around it was secured with a tiny silver buckle. Brenda then retrieved another envelope and placed it next to the bag. Mac watched as she looked intently for more items.

"It looks like this is it," he said. "Which do you want to open first?"

"Let's go for the bag first. The letter in the second envelope may tell us the meaning of its contents."

Inside the leather bag, she could tell there were multiple things, even something quite heavy, but the first thing she felt was something like jewelry. She pulled out a silver filigree locket in the shape of a heart, tarnished but beautiful. Brenda turned the heart-shaped locket over. Carefully, she opened it to see pictures of a man on one side and a woman on the other side. She studied the clothing they wore and their facial expressions before handing it to Mac.

"It looks like the photos were taken sometime in the 1970s," he said. "I wonder who they are." Brenda shook her head wonderingly and then reached inside the leather pouch again. She quickly withdrew her hand. "What's wrong?" Mac asked. She handed the bag to him. He reached in and immediately knew the next find was a pistol.

Brenda peered over his shoulder as he read the words "Lettie Mackey c. 1890" engraved on the handle. The pistol was a small one that easily fit a woman's hand. "The mystery deepens," Brenda said uneasily. "We find 1970s photos and a pistol dated 1890—I don't get it. Let's see what else is in there." She reached in for the last item and pulled out a muslin bag, somewhat yellowed. Inside were a handful of gold coins. "None of this makes sense," she said.

Mac fingered the coins. "They are old, too. I would say they are probably quite valuable, but I'm no expert. Maybe you should read the letter next. I have a feeling we'll learn much more after that."

Brenda had almost forgotten the other envelope and carefully unsealed it. The handwriting varied, in that the written letters were irregular. Brenda began to read it aloud to Mac.

The contents of this box are evidence of a crime committed in Sweetfern Harbor in 1982. The Mackey's inherited a family home and the killer wanted what they had. He broke in, not realizing the couple was home. He overpowered them and killed them. He managed to take these valuables with him. I know who did it because he showed them to me. I stole them from him to protect the evidence of his heinous crime. He got away with murder.

Brenda's eyes grew wide and she and Mac sat silent at first.

"If this note states the truth, then we have found evidence of a crime, Brenda."

Brenda snapped open the locket again. "Do you think these two are the victims? If so, why would the killer take a locket with their photos in it?"

"I'll have it checked out. Perhaps the necklace itself is a valuable heirloom."

The detective knew he would open a cold case file with this evidence. The crime was unfamiliar to him, but the year given would afford him a head start with details. Brenda wanted to talk about the possibilities that flooded her mind. Brenda was also a member of the police force, courtesy of his boss Chief Bob Ingram, though due to her duties at the bed and breakfast she identified herself as a member on-call only.

"I have so many questions," Brenda said. "I agree it must be that the locket holds the value and not necessarily the photos in it. It also sounds as if whoever wrote this note may not have played a part in it all, beyond hiding the evidence. Why didn't they say something to the police back then?" She noticed the leather bag. "This looks very old. Maybe the pistol belongs inside it."

Brenda told Mac she wanted to discover more about the woman from the 1890s who owned it. Mac was musing about the possibilities, too.

"Many women during those times owned guns. The country was wild and they were taught how to use them for protection." Mac often thought Brenda could benefit having one of her own, but she was against the idea. She had explained how rattled she would be if ever confronting a burglar, stating she would probably end up shooting herself anyway. Mac could see from Brenda's reluctant expression that she thought he was bringing up the topic so he could remind her about the idea. "I'm not going to suggest again that you should have one, Brenda. I'm just saying it was different in those times. Often, women were in their homes alone with their children while the men worked the land, or herded cattle to markets. It was common for them to learn protection. Maybe Lettie Mackey lived out West, or in California during the Gold Rush."

Brenda considered this. "When you get any information at all, call me right away, Mac. I find this case intriguing."

They carefully put the items back into the box. Mac took the skeleton key and locked it. They talked a while longer until they noticed the hour. Mac suggested they get a good night's sleep and talk again in the morning.

Brenda's last thoughts before falling asleep were of the mysterious box buried in the grounds of Sheffield Bed and Breakfast. Mac was just as interested in delving into it as she was.

After breakfast the next morning, Phyllis and Brenda sipped coffee alone before beginning their day.

"Is William busy today?" she asked Phyllis.

"I think he plans to work on the venue for the upcoming business convention with a guest of ours. Logan Clark? He is here to set up initial layouts. William and the city council will do the rest. Do you want to see him?"

"I just have a quick question for him. I can just give him a quick call and not take up a lot of his time."

Phyllis didn't question her. She knew William and the archaeologist had met with the contractor regarding historic architecture and design, and presumed that was the subject of Brenda's inquiry. They finished their usual morning get-together and Brenda went outside to talk with Rich Turner.

"Mac and I were curious last night and poked around the area where you said you felt something hard. It wasn't a rock. We found an old metal chest and got it out."

Rich stared at her. "How did you manage without heavy machinery?"

"It wasn't buried as deeply as we first thought. It took some work but we managed. It was a small item, just heavy, and we brought it inside." She hoped her smile told him it had been no big deal.

"I hope it brings you riches, Brenda."

She laughed nervously. "There were a few things in it, but I don't know about riches. My uncle was an avid collector of antiques and various artifacts. Three or four of the items looked like some I've found in the attic in his old trunks."

Her casual attitude told Rich there must not have been anything of significance.

"I think I should go ahead with the excavator to make sure nothing else is down there."

Brenda agreed. She thought there was a possibility of something else in the ground but didn't want to voice her thoughts. "If you do find the buried treasure, let me know," she said. Rich agreed and motioned for the operator to begin with the backhoe. Brenda returned to the bed and breakfast.

Phyllis met her near the kitchen. "William happened to call. He said to tell you he's coming over here anyway and will see you then. Is this about the house design?"

There was no way Brenda could keep the news from her best friend and most valued employee. "Mac and I found a buried chest out there last night. It was buried down in the dirt, but not so deep a little muscle didn't dig it up."

A man stopped in his tracks and eavesdropped on the conversation. His heart quickened and he regretted ever thinking the object would remain buried forever. Never in his wildest dreams would he have thought more construction would ensue on the premises. He wiped his hands on his pants and hurried down the hall when the conversation came to a close. He hadn't counted on the owner of Sheffield Bed and Breakfast marrying a lead detective either.

A few minutes later, Brenda observed Rich Turner berating his assistant Andy Shelton. The opened window allowed words to reach their ears. Andy Shelton had just arrived late for work and was threatened with losing his job if it happened again.

Brenda hoped Rich's way of handling differences wouldn't interfere with the progress of the new home.

chapter three

An hour before dinner that evening, Annette Pickard asked Allie if Brenda was in her office.

"She is," Allie said, surprised by Annette's somber tone. "Do you want to talk to her?" Annette nodded.

Allie called Brenda to tell her Annette wanted to speak with her. Brenda told her to send her in. When Brenda stood to greet her, she noted the ashen face of the guest before her. She asked Annette if she felt all right.

"I'm fine, but I feel I must discuss something that is disturbing to me." Brenda encouraged her to continue. "Logan Clark unnerves me, and I wondered if it is all right if I change places in the dining room for meals."

"If any guest is bothering you I will handle it immediately. As for changing places, no one has assigned seating at the table or anywhere in the bed and breakfast. You are free to sit wherever you wish. What is Mr. Clark doing that is upsetting to you?"

The writer shook her head. "It's just that he looks at me

in a way that makes me uncomfortable. He seems to be scrutinizing me for some reason."

"I'll be glad to talk with him."

"I mainly just wanted you to be aware of how I'm feeling. Please don't say anything to him. There is nothing concrete I can say against him and I don't want to disturb the tranquility here."

"If that is the way you want it, I'll respect your wishes. Please let me know right away if the matter escalates. I have no intention of allowing one guest to unsettle another." Brenda watched her as she first began to stand up, but then hesitated and sat back down.

"I appreciate your understanding," Annette said. Brenda felt the guest had more to say but instead, her guest hastily stood up and thanked her, backing out of the office.

"Would you like to get away for a bit and take a walk downtown with Phyllis and me?"

Annette declined and stated she had to get back to her writing.

Once Annette returned to her room, Brenda gathered Allie and Phyllis. She told them of the conversation and advised them to be on the alert for anything that appeared suspicious about Logan Clark's manner toward Annette Pickard.

"I haven't noticed anything unusual about him," Allie said, "but I do think Annette is a little strange. Maybe it's all in her head."

"Either way, we have to take notice." Brenda told them to keep it under wraps. "Try not to be obvious."

The two young couples came downstairs, their voices

audible before they were visible. Josh Meyers told Brenda she had given them a good lead when she suggested Jonathan Wright. It seemed Jon had taken the guests under his wing and they had really enjoyed one of the pontoon boats he rented.

"These two like to dive, and we do, too," Lauren said, "but the skies were so beautiful that Holly and I took advantage and soaked up the sun."

"Are you going out for more?" Allie asked.

"Lauren and I are going shopping. We haven't had time to look at all the cute little shops downtown." Holly swung her bag over her shoulder. "I'm sure Josh and Clint will go back and harass Jonathan again." She turned to the two men. "Don't forget to meet us at four at Morning Sun Coffee. I hear it's been around for a long time and serves delicious drinks and food." Josh and Clint assured them they would catch up.

"Phyllis and I are getting ready to walk downtown," Brenda said. "Her daughter is the owner of Morning Sun Coffee, in fact. We'll introduce you to Molly. You might be interested to know that she and Jon Wright are dating."

The women were delighted and agreed to join them. They mentioned how they had enjoyed meeting the boat and watersports rental man and were pleased to hear that Phyllis's daughter had found happiness with such a nice person. "I guess she's found her Mr. Right—well, make that Mr. W-r-i-g-h-t?" Lauren giggled at her own joke and everyone laughed.

"He's very well liked around town, and everyone calls him Jon," Phyllis said. "I'm sure he would be happy for you to shorten his name. He told us he considers Jonathan too formal." Her eyes held good humor.

They chatted about places of interest as they walked along the street. When they came to Jenny's Blossoms, Brenda suggested she introduce them to her step-daughter. "Jenny came with the package when I married Mac. She is a wonderful daughter and owns this flower shop. She is also married to a detective."

Jenny finished a transaction and smiled when she saw Brenda and Phyllis walk in. The two women with them were approximately her age. They were introduced and the newcomers admired her window display. "The flowers in here are beautiful," Holly said. Jenny thanked her and told them she hoped they were enjoying their stay at the bed and breakfast and in the village.

"We're going to hit every shop on the street and then our husbands will join us at the coffee shop later. At least they promised they'd be on time," Lauren said.

"We're hoping they'll be ready for a cool drink by then," Holly said. Lauren agreed that food and drink were the only things that could drag their husbands away from the water.

"Bryce and I plan to eat at the Italian restaurant down the street tonight," Jenny said. "I highly recommend it. If the four of you want to join us, you are welcome to."

Brenda noted the enthusiasm in their faces. "I'll take your names off the list for dinner at the bed and breakfast tonight if you want to go with them." They thanked her and then told Jenny they'd meet at the restaurant at seven. Jenny explained where to find it and said she'd make a reservation.

Entering Morning Sun Coffee down the street, Brenda noticed Jane and Logan Clark sitting at a table near the window. Everyone greeted one another as if they were old friends. Molly approached the tables and was introduced. Jane commented on the delicious latte she had indulged in and Logan told her he had never enjoyed a chicken wrap like Molly's. Molly told him all ingredients were organic and locally grown. Jane was even more interested.

"I am happy to know you use organic ingredients. That explains your delicious, fresh food." Other than those words, Jane Clark said little, but Brenda could tell she seemed to relax more as the hours of her stay in Sweetfern Harbor continued. Molly thanked her for the compliment and then took orders from the rest of the newcomers.

Brenda discreetly observed Logan in particular and saw nothing amiss in his mannerisms.

"Where are the two of you from?" Holly asked. She directed her question at the Clarks.

"We're from New York City," Logan said.

"We love going to New York, especially during the holiday season," Lauren said. "When we can convince Josh and Clint to come along, we take in a show once in a while. Have you lived there long?"

"We moved there a few years after our marriage," Logan said. "So we've been there nine or ten years now." Brenda noticed that would make them relatively newlyweds, though they were in their late forties; she didn't question it since she and Mac married in their mid to late forties as well. Sensing the younger women's curiosity, Logan said, "The marriage is a first one for both of us." Jane frowned at his comment. Obviously she didn't feel the need to explain their private lives.

The conversation moved to highlights of the town's attractions. Molly told them about various places of interest. Logan and Jane excused themselves and left the coffee shop.

Once outside, Logan mentioned another guest to his wife. "Do you know of anyone with the last name of Pickard?" Jane told him one of the guests had that name. "I realize that. I believe I may have heard that name before."

Jane nudged him. "I'm sure you have, Logan. You're in the textile business and must meet many people. It wouldn't be unusual to meet someone in your travels with that last name."

He agreed with her and changed the subject. Though outwardly he brushed it off, his mind raced. He knew that last name very well and wondered if Annette Pickard was related. He must find out. He hadn't missed the unnerved look on her face when he asked her name. Treading carefully was in order. He followed his wife into Jenny's Blossoms. Ahead of them was a man in a police uniform.

"Well, what brings my handsome detective in here?" the owner asked with a sweet smile. She accepted the officer's brief kiss and turned to her customers. A faint tint of red crept into her face when she realized they were strangers. "This is my husband, Detective Bryce Jones," she said. "I'm Jenny, the owner here."

The Clarks introduced themselves. Logan stood back, slightly behind his wife's shoulder, gazing around at the displays. Bryce glanced at him only because he appeared to hang back. Jane asked about the source of Jenny's flowers and was told when in season, all were grown locally in gardens.

"Otherwise, I order them from an organic nursery not far from here." Jenny and Jane were caught up in a conversation about flowers. The two men waited patiently, not looking at one another.

"Jenny," Bryce said, "I stopped to say hello, but I have a desk piled with several cases that are waiting to be solved. I'll catch you later."

"Wait a minute, Bryce. We're meeting new friends at the Italian restaurant at seven tonight. I hope you won't have to work late."

He waved and promised he'd be home in time.

"I'm afraid we interrupted your visit," Jane said.

"Bryce and I know our jobs are demanding, and I am here for my customers first. I'm happy you dropped in." She directed Jane to the new shipment of roses. "These were ordered for Sheffield Bed and Breakfast specifically. The owners are my parents. I've always delivered only the very best to Brenda, even before she married my father."

Jenny's melodious laugh was contagious, and Jane's demeanor relaxed. She related well to the young owner of Jenny's Blossoms. Logan grew even tenser. The Sheffield Bed and Breakfast was entwined with officers of the law in more ways than one and he began to regret coming back to the area. It hadn't been easy to convince Jane to spend a long weekend in a small harbor town. He should be happy she was getting into the spirit of the environment, but now he wished she hated every minute of their trip.

When Logan saw Jane admiring a pink rose he decided

to buy it for her. She protested at first, telling him she had no way to keep it fresh. Jenny told her the bed and breakfast had plenty of bud vases and they had only to ask.

"Sweetfern Harbor hosts many events throughout the year and Brenda keeps all kinds of extra things around. She will surely have a vase for you. She entertains often, plus events often hold after-parties or concluding galas at Sheffield Bed and Breakfast."

Logan paid for the rose and together he and Jane walked back to the bed and breakfast.

"I'm really surprised, Logan. I had no idea how much this area would grow on me." She stopped and looked up the drive at the majestic Queen Anne. "I'd love to know the intimate history of this place, wouldn't you?"

Logan swallowed twice and said, "I like history, but I doubt anything unusual happened around here. I mean, it's probably like all Victorian structures with the usual histories."

"I wonder if it has any ghosts, or maybe a murder occurred here, or some other juicy tidbits of crime."

Logan looked at his wife and wondered what had brought out this side of her. Ordinarily, Jane was reserved and concentrated on designing unique household items that only the rich and famous could afford. He had never realized she could be so interested in things of the past, much less sinister histories. They continued to the front door.

Annette Pickard began to descend the stairs. Her eyes met Logan's and she looked away quickly. She heard Allie Williams greet the couple and felt it was safe enough to continue downstairs. Voices floated from the kitchen when she went into the guest snack nook. She poured hot water into a teacup and dipped a raspberry tea bag into it and turned to go back to her room. Once she finished writing the last chapter, she planned to take a walk down to the ocean before the editing process began. Despite the look on Logan's face just now, she felt she had made a narrow escape. She stopped to add honey to her tea before she returned to her room.

As his wife Jane carried on a light conversation with Allie, Logan decided Annette would be more receptive in this friendly environment than if he caught her alone. He greeted her in a friendly voice. She mumbled good afternoon and almost stumbled in surprise as she turned toward the stairs.

"Have you written other books, Miss Pickard?" Logan asked her. She shook her head slightly. "Where are they listed? My wife likes to read mysteries."

Annette told him where to find her books. When she mentioned several bookstores in the town she came from, his attention perked up. She was from Pennsylvania and in fact, from a town he knew well. He scrutinized her face briefly and saw no signs of recognition. Jane turned toward them when Allie seemed particularly interested in their conversation.

"It's true, Miss Pickard, that I read mysteries when I have rare downtime." Flustered, Annette repeated the names of a few bookstores, including online stores, when Jane asked. "I'll order one or two while I'm here. Once back home, my life will pick up to a fast pace again."

When Logan hesitated to accompany her to their room,

Jane noticed he wanted to say more to the writer. He smiled at his wife and walked with her to the stairs. Allie watched Annette who lingered at the snack nook, stirring her tea, and didn't go upstairs.

"I think I'll have my tea in the sitting room," she told Allie. Allie offered to bring fresh cookies for her but Annette declined. Allie made a mental note to relate the interchange to Brenda.

When the Clarks got to their door, Logan hung back as if waiting for something. Jane went inside and once Logan realized Annette hadn't followed them upstairs, he shrugged his shoulders and followed Jane. She opened her laptop and searched for books by Annette Pickard. Logan stretched out on the bed and fell asleep, tired by the long day of walking.

Jane read more about Annette and she stopped scrolling when she saw the name Hal Pickard. She started to ask Logan what he knew about the man, but didn't when she saw that he had fallen asleep. She recalled that name from years ago before she met and married Logan although she couldn't remember any details. Perhaps when he woke he could help her remember why the name seemed so familiar.

chapter four

Mac sat at his office desk and poured over the cold case file. His instincts told him he would find information about the 1982 murders that had not been properly investigated at the time. The fact that it was a cold case didn't surprise him that much. He hadn't heard gossip about the event around town and only vaguely recalled hearing about an unsolved murder before he joined the department. He sat upright when he read the last name Mackey. He reached for his phone.

"Brenda, if you have a few minutes, you may want to come down to my office. I've found some interesting news about an unsolved murder from 1982."

"I'm on my way."

Brenda and Phyllis had just arrived home. She was in the kitchen telling Morgan to remove four from the dinner count when Mac called. Her heart beat a little faster as she headed out the back door and got into her car. She felt sure his news had something to do with the metal chest that held the assortment of items.

Mac greeted her with a quick kiss and they both sat down. Brenda sat on the edge of the chair and Mac shuffled several papers. The metal chest was sitting on the desk, next to a file storage box which read *Cold Case: Mackey – 1982*.

"Bridget and Thomas Mackey lived in a very nice home that Thomas inherited from his wealthy mother when she died. His mother had been married, then divorced when she took her maiden name of Mackey back. She changed her sons name to Mackey as well, to preserve a part of his inheritance. The property had come from her parents originally. Everyone seemed to like young Thomas and Bridget Mackey, according to the notes here. The townspeople were aware that a home like that had valuables in it, but Sweetfern Harbor rarely saw crime. So it was a shock to find out that someone had broken into the home to steal priceless items. It was even more of a shock when the bodies of the young couple were discovered."

"What leads did they have?"

"The neighbors were all questioned and no one had heard or seen anything amiss. The next door neighbor, whose home was situated some distance away from theirs mentioned a handyman who worked over there regularly. One neighbor who knew Bridget well said the woman told her that the handyman was asked at times to do minor work inside the home, as well."

Brenda asked for the name. Mac told her that no one seemed to recall the man's name and said he hadn't been seen during the two weeks before the break-in and murder.

"It's hard to believe they couldn't track him down," Brenda said.

"They attempted to, but failed. Neither Bridget nor Thomas ever complained about him to anyone. It seemed he was a trustworthy person. I guess they didn't pursue it much further than that. He probably didn't live right in town, he could have lived in any number of the small towns and villages up and down the coast, travelling around looking for odd jobs." Mac pulled the metal box closer and opened it. "The coins are Greek. I have a coin dealer expert coming in today to provide more information. They could have been collected long ago by someone in the Mackey family. I'm sure they enjoyed their wealth and could easily travel around the world."

Brenda's eyes landed on the leather bag that held the small pistol. She regretted there was no way to meet the fearless woman who had owned it. "How much is that pistol worth?"

"This small revolver, in today's market, is worth in the thousands. Lettie Mackey probably paid around eight or nine dollars for it back in her day. That was an expensive sum in her time. The silver locket is with the appraiser now, but at first glance he felt it was heirloom quality and also quite valuable."

"I would say whoever robbed them knew what they had and where the items were kept." Brenda frowned. "Unless the robber had reason to kill them, I'm surprised he broke in when they were home."

They tossed a few ideas around until Brenda asked to

read over the notes taken on the case in 1982 and beyond. She saw that Bridget and Thomas had children, daughters Lacy and Mae. Both lived in upstate New York. The Mackey home had remained intact but vacant ever since the murders. She presumed the daughters had long since retrieved anything of value. Brenda continued reading until Mac was called to Chief Ingram's office on another matter. Brenda stayed in Mac's office and read reports. Her eyes caught a sentence that caused her to sit upright.

The name Hal Pickard struck her. The notes mentioned he had been interrogated three times in the early days and allowed to leave without being arrested. He had been highly suspected since he knew the handyman well, but claimed he did not know the man's name. Hal also had a history of crime-related activities, though no felonies, and none as serious as murder. The prison gates were like swinging doors for him.

Brenda didn't have time to read more. Her phone rang and she was needed at the bed and breakfast. Two employees in the kitchen had suddenly became ill and her chef had needed to send them home. Brenda always filled in when a crisis occurred. Mac returned to his office and told her he hadn't had time to read through everything on the case yet and he would see her at dinnertime to discuss what they had learned.

The last name Pickard stuck in Brenda's mind as she drove home. As soon as her day ended she vowed to get on her laptop and start researching one guest's name in particular. How was Hal related to Annette? In the meantime, she donned an apron and pitched in to help

Morgan through the busy dinner preparation. They chattered as they worked like two school girls.

"I really appreciate your help, Brenda," Morgan said. "I hope the two girls just have a minor virus and nothing spreads around the bed and breakfast."

"Check on them again later when things slow down, Morgan. So far I haven't heard of anyone else falling ill. Those two are good friends. They may have eaten something away from here that didn't settle well."

The chef shook her head. "I don't know how they can eat some of the things they do. Tacos from down at that new little shack-like café seem to be a favorite with them. Slushy drinks at that new drive-in place at all hours of the night. They probably picked something up there."

Dinner was served on time. Phyllis stayed around to help Brenda serve and then they both sat down with the guests until time for dessert. Brenda was anxious to get to her computer. She glanced across the table at Annette and smiled at her. The writer returned a brief smile. As had been her habit, Annette ate very little. Brenda was tempted to ask her if she knew anyone named Hal Pickard, but didn't dare, since if anything embarrassing unfolded she didn't want to make her guest uncomfortable. Brenda breathed evenly knowing both Clarks sat at the opposite end of the table away from Annette.

When it was time for dessert, Annette excused herself and went to her room. Logan moved as if to follow her and then changed his mind when Brenda piped up to ask him a question about his day in town. Annette may have something to worry about after all, thought Brenda. Allie had reported the exchange earlier and now she wondered what was going on between the two guests. For now, at least, she had distracted Logan from harassing Annette any further.

Annette settled down to her laptop, opened up the novel and started editing. The narrative would be sold as fiction, though she based it on bits and pieces of stories told by her embittered mother over the years. She had no idea if her mother recounted facts or made-up tales against her father because of the strained and abusive relationship between them. All she knew is that it made for a fascinating story.

Annette would get the editing done but knew the book wouldn't be finished until one more task was completed. Her mother had written piles of notes to Annette over the years, scribbling angry missives inside holiday cards. The holidays never failed to make her mother miserable with remembered bits of life from her time with that man. "I'm putting things in writing for you, Annette, so you will never forget how rotten your father is," she would write. Her mother had no idea that Annette had kept the scraggly handwritten notes for the purpose of her stories.

Before she closed her laptop and started for the shower, Logan Clark came to mind. Annette didn't doubt he desperately wanted to have a longer conversation with her, but there was no way she planned to allow that. There was nothing sexual or overtly bad about his approach, but his mannerisms caused her to shiver with aversion nonetheless. Though she lived well enough, Logan and his wife were obviously very rich people. She tried to think of just one thing about herself that might interest Logan Clark, aside from his exhaustingly dull questions about where to buy her books. Her mind went blank. Surely he was just being a bore. The rushing water that showered her washed away thoughts of the Clarks.

The next morning, Mac was up early and went downstairs to grab a quick breakfast in the kitchen. He and the chef spoke briefly. Brenda was disappointed to learn he hadn't gotten much further in the notes on the Mackey murders.

Brenda, Phyllis and Allie all noted that Annette Pickard lingered downstairs a bit longer. She had asked them for the shortest pathway to the ocean and Phyllis directed her.

"Watch your step during the first part because there is some loose rock. After that, you'll reach the sand." Phyllis continued to speak of how beautiful the Atlantic Ocean was, especially in the morning. The smile Annette gave her was the first full one any of them had noticed.

"She's really very pretty, especially when she smiles," Brenda said, after the door closed behind the guest.

"I still think there is something mysterious about her," Allie said.

Logan Clark came from the sitting room and appeared to be in a hurry. "Logan, wait and I'll go with you," Jane said. She caught up with her husband who displayed a mild scowl of impatience. "I said I'd like to walk down to the water with you. Is there a problem with that?"

"There's no problem, Jane. I may not be good company since I have some things on my mind about business. But, come along."

Jane stood back and her face hardened. "I know when you don't want me with you, Logan. I'll catch up later." She turned on her heel and stomped up the stairs.

Brenda and Phyllis exchanged glances when they saw Logan hurry as if to catch up with Annette. At that same moment, William Pendleton came through the front door and into the lobby. He kissed his wife Phyllis on the cheek and greeted Allie and Brenda. He explained he was there to give more information to Rich Turner and started for the back passageway.

"Let's go down to the ocean first, William," Phyllis said. She grabbed her husband's arm and pulled him toward the door.

Confused, he asked her if she didn't have the usual morning work to do. He glanced over his shoulder at Brenda who shrugged her shoulders. She and Allie went into the sitting room and watched until all were out of sight.

"Phyllis will get to the bottom of what Logan wants from Annette," Allie said.

The bell rang at the desk and both women returned to the front lobby to see Jenny loading roses inside. Hope Williams followed her friend with a large tray of freshly baked scones and bagels from the bakery.

"The roses are beautiful, but it's hard to resist the smell of those delicious goodies, Mom," Allie said. "I love it when the Sweet Treats deliveries arrive." She took the tray from Hope and carried them to the kitchen, though not before Brenda told her to keep her fingers out of them.

"You know I can't resist tasting one now."

Hope went back to Jenny's van and they brought in the last of the flower order. Jenny proceeded to arrange them around the bed and breakfast on the first floor. "I thought roses would be something different for a change. I hope you like them, Brenda."

Brenda assured her they were beautiful. "I like the idea of having them around since this will be the last day for some of the guests. The scent is heavenly."

She invited the women to join her in the sitting room for a taste of Sweet Treats goodies. "I took out four of them before I took them to the kitchen," Allie said. She went into the dining room and brought the small tray to them while the others filled their coffee and tea cups. They settled in the cushiony furniture and talked about the early morning happenings around town.

"I think the upcoming business convention will bring a lot of customers into the shops," Hope said. "I've already told my two extra helpers to count on working most of that weekend."

"We're booked up here," Allie said "I'm glad William is so interested in finding opportunities to bring in tourists and others."

The subject switched to Allie's recent paintings. Allie had a reserved spot on the convention floor for them.

"Your dad convinced the radio station and TV channel to broadcast your paintings for sale," Hope said. David Williams was a popular local news anchor and managed to twist arms in his favor when it came to his daughter and her artistic talent.

William and Phyllis made their way down the slope to the ocean. "What's your hurry, Phyllis?" William asked. She didn't answer and took his hand. "Knowing you, you must have had a good reason to come down here this hour of the morning."

"We're following two of our guests," she said. Phyllis explained the recent encounters between Logan Clark and Annette Pickard.

Logan was just a few steps behind Annette, and the Pendleton's had gained steps as well. Annette turned as if ascertaining who was behind her. She stopped and even in the early sunlight Phyllis saw her face whiten. They slowed their pace when closer to the two guests. A few other people were on the beach, scattered along the sand and the rocks, or jogging at the edge of the waves.

"I know someone with the same last name as you," Logan said. Annette didn't answer. Phyllis pulled William to a stop, just within earshot, and pretended to gaze off in a different direction. "It's an innocent question. Surely you can tell me if you are related to Hal Pickard."

Annette turned on her heel and started back toward Sheffield Bed and Breakfast. When Logan started to grab her arm, William dropped the pretense and stepped in.

"It seems the young lady doesn't want to answer your questions. She is a guest of the bed and breakfast and is here to relax." William's tone held an authority Phyllis hadn't heard before.

Logan looked at them and when he recognized Phyllis, attempted an explanation. "I simply wanted to ask if she is related to someone I know who has the same last name. I don't believe that is harassment."

"It isn't unless the lady doesn't want to speak with you and you persist." Phyllis recalled her husband had been the captain of a small cruise ship long ago, which explained his almost military tone.

William turned and Phyllis followed him back to the

bed and breakfast. By that point, Annette was almost to the front door. Logan remained on the sand gazing at the rippling waters.

The four women in the sitting room heard quick footsteps and saw only a flash of Annette Pickard as she entered and hurried upstairs to her room. Phyllis and William joined them and related the event near the ocean.

"I'll have a talk with Logan Clark," Brenda said, "and find out what's going on." She went to the front entrance and sat at Allie's desk to wait for Logan. When he came in, she told him she must speak to him.

"I was simply curious about her last name," he said. "I knew someone in the past with the same surname and wondered if she was related."

Brenda became more alert. "How exactly did you know this other person with the same name?"

"I remember visiting Sweetfern Harbor years ago when I was young. My parents brought me here for vacations twice. One year, there was someone named Hal Pickard who was suspected of killing a wealthy couple who lived in the town. I just remember his name. I guess when one hears such things in their youth it's easy to remember."

Brenda scrutinized his face. "Please leave your fellow guests alone. Everyone comes here for peace and quiet, or to enjoy attractions around town. It's plain that Annette is not happy to be asked questions and I don't allow my guests to upset each other."

Logan set his jaw and promised to keep his distance. After he left, Brenda calculated the approximate age Logan Clark would have been in 1982. She caught him before he got to the first step. "How old were you when your parents brought you here for vacations?"

He appeared to think back. "I was in my early teens, I suppose." His eyes wandered from her face. "That was a long time ago, since I'm in my early fifties now." He gave a short laugh and proceeded upstairs.

Brenda calculated that in 1982, Logan Clark would have been past his early teens, probably late teens. She knew that if what he told her was true, his story about his parents bringing him to Sweetfern Harbor as a child for family vacations didn't quite add up. Phyllis had gone upstairs to begin cleaning the rooms of guests who had left for the day. William had gone to talk with Rich Turner. Brenda knew there was nothing more she could do at Sheffield House and was determined to figure out how Logan Clark fit into the story. She told Allie she would be back later and could be reached at the police station.

Detective Mac Rivers looked up with pleasure on his face when he saw Brenda come in. She told him to drop everything because she had news for him. When she finished telling him of the events of the morning, he clasped his hands behind his head and leaned back in his chair.

"Logan Clark is someone I want to talk to right away, Brenda. It could be that the key to solving this cold case is right there in Sheffield Bed and Breakfast." He reached for the phone and Allie answered in a cheerful voice. Mac instructed her to tell the guest to come down to the police station right away, and Allie hung up and called up to Logan's room.

However, there was no answer. Allie went upstairs just

in time to see the Clarks emerge from their room. Apparently, they were still feuding and had ignored the ringing phone. She heard Jane tell her husband in a wounded voice that she would see him that evening. She planned to spend the day in the shops and was interested in the local museum. Allie waited an awkward moment and then gave Logan the message from the detective. His eyes darted everywhere except to her face.

"He said to come down as soon as possible."

Logan Clark wiped moisture from his forehead and nodded. He mentally kicked himself for ever getting near Annette Pickard.

chapter five

F
ar from Sheffield Bed and Breakfast, a person who knew far too much about the 1982 murders was enjoying a nap when he was rudely awakened by a loud knocking sound. "Pickard, you have a visitor," said a voice after rapping again on the metal door.

Hal Pickard woke up on his hard prison cot and looked at the guard with surprise. It was a rare occasion when anyone took an interest in him. Before his latest incarceration, he was often approached by journalists and other media outlets. Hal knew how to outsmart all of them when they questioned him about past deeds. The one they were most interested in was the murder of Bridgett and Thomas Mackey. They always apologized before the interviews, stating they realized he was only a suspect. His concern had always centered on his loot. The lock on his dingy apartment was flimsy. When he came back from the tavern after celebrating his good luck, he flopped on the flat mattress and slept until the next morning. That was when he discovered the missing valuables intended to set him up for a lifetime. He was forced to revert to petty crimes to earn his way, after that.

Living inside the prison walls wasn't too bad as the years passed. The lifers got to know him and he was a likeable prisoner. Most admired him for his ability to be released on a regular basis. He taught the younger ones who were in for short periods to always keep crimes below the radar as much as possible.

Accompanied by a guard, he walked to the visiting room, expecting to see a reporter who got wind of his recent attempted bank robbery. He anticipated the diversion. The guard became alert when Hal stopped and stared at the woman sitting there.

"Hello, Hal," Mattie said. He shuffled forward and sat down across from his estranged wife.

"I almost didn't recognize you, Mattie. What are you doing here?"

"I came to tell you there may be a book coming out about you." She noted his satisfied smile. "It won't be flattering, Hal."

"Who's writing it and how do you know about it?"

"Never mind who is writing it. As to how I know, I keep close tabs on the author—from a distance, of course. The author has first-hand knowledge about you." She smirked a little and started to stand up.

"Is that all you came for, Mattie? You could have called instead of coming all the way out here."

"I wanted to see your expression when I told you." She could see now that he was proud of the fact that someone was writing a book about him. "Like I told you, there won't be anything pretty in it." Her voice lowered in scorn as she sneered. Hal shrugged, unimpressed, and waited for her to say something more interesting. It seemed that was all, however.

When Hal got back to his cell, he shrugged his shoulders again. Mattie had once attracted him with her youthful beauty. Her petty anger had caused lines to settle and deepen in her face that didn't flatter her. He wondered about her motive for telling him face to face. Plenty of stuff had been written about him over the years, though not recently. He liked the idea that he still caught the interest of the public and planned to tell everyone he knew inside. Mattie had done him a favor in boosting his mood to face another day in the dismal surroundings of life behind bars.

Mattie smiled to herself as she got into her car. When the whim hit her to antagonize Hal Pickard she knew just how to surprise him after all these years. Never would she forget his treatment of her. She was aware he had committed petty crimes during the few short years of their marriage. Hal Pickard had never held down a decent job in the years she knew him. Mattie found it hard to recall just what it was that attracted her in the first place, unless it was his pure recklessness. She was no angel herself in those days. Hal had contributed in large part to making her the embittered woman she became.

She felt satisfied she gave him something to boast about that would never transpire in his lifetime. Journalists had long ago forgotten that despicable man. It was her way of putting bait out to feed his egotistical mind, and to torment him. She expected him to brag about the book to other inmates. In the end, he would be the laughingstock of the prison.

Logan Clark walked into the police station and was directed to the detective's office. He saw Brenda Rivers sitting there and wondered if she had reported him for asking questions of the writer. He was well aware that was no crime, and bristled at her nosiness. "So what is Ms. Rivers doing here?" he asked.

"You may not be aware of it, but Brenda is authorized on the police force here in Sweetfern Harbor. She doesn't work with us full-time but serves on-call." The detective then motioned for Logan to sit down. Mac called Bryce to join them.

"This is Detective Bryce Jones," Mac said.

Logan squirmed in his chair and shifted to find a comfortable position. The law surrounded him in this town, something he didn't expect when he booked a room at the Sheffield Bed and Breakfast. He closed his fists, hoping his skin would suck in the moisture that slicked his palms and nodded at the young detective, acknowledging the introduction, wondering if the detective would remember they'd already met at the florist shop.

"You spoke earlier with Brenda about youthful visits to Sweetfern Harbor," Mac said. "I'd like to know when you were in our town."

"My parents brought me here twice that I recall. We all enjoyed the ocean and especially sail boating. It was probably when I was in my early teens."

"Would you say you visited sometime in the nineteen-eighties?"

"It was a long time ago, but yes, I believe it was

sometime in that decade." Mac asked him his present age and he said he was fifty-four. Logan turned to Brenda and produced a crooked smile. "Forgive me, miss, I didn't want to tell you my exact age since I don't like to admit I'm aging."

Brenda secretly admired the man for keeping fit. He certainly didn't look in his fifties. Mac seemed to be far away in his thoughts for a few seconds. "I calculate that in the eighties, you were past your early teens. Are you sure your parents brought you here for vacations when you were a teenager?"

Logan thought fast. "You're right. I must have come on my own later, before going to college. It was between my high school graduation and first year of college. When I came with my parents I was much younger. There weren't as many tourists around here as I recall."

Before he could change the subject, Bryce asked the next question. "Did you vacation here, or settle in Sweetfern Harbor?"

"I vacationed only. I had to get my college education. My parents were determined I have that."

Brenda asked him what college he graduated from and his degree. He stumbled a second or two and then regained control. He mentioned a small college in Massachusetts and told her his degree was in marketing. Mac made a note of his answer.

"Do you recall a case of two murders here in 1982?"

Logan met Mac's penetrating stare. "I remember reading about something like that, but I was pretty young. It didn't really interest me. Like I said, I was on my way to college and that pretty well superseded everything else."

When the detective told him he would like to question him in depth at a later time, Logan protested, stating he had business to get back to. He and Jane were due back in New York the next afternoon. Mac told him he would try to get back to him in time. They all stood and the detective thanked him for his cooperation.

They watched Logan from the side window of Mac's office until he sped away.

"He is adept at lying and then just as easily explains his lies," Brenda said.

"I'll look into that college," Bryce said. He took the notepad from Mac and left to make a phone call and move forward with the investigation.

"I'm going to research Logan Clark," Brenda said. "I think there's more to him than he is letting on. I wonder if he ever came here as a child at all. And something tells me he knows this town better than he's letting on."

"That doesn't mean he is a criminal of any kind, Brenda. It could be he is a very private person and doesn't like anyone delving into his personal life."

"Right, Mac." He didn't miss the light sarcasm in her tone. She kissed him and left for the bed and breakfast.

The two employees were well again and returned to the kitchen, and Brenda waved to Morgan when she stopped in to see them. She told the two girls she was happy they didn't have anything serious. Her chef rolled her eyes behind their backs. Brenda asked for a boxed lunch to take upstairs with her.

"If you need me, I'll be in our apartment." Morgan packed her a fresh sandwich with turkey and avocado and a side salad, with a bottle of water tucked into a handled bag like they always did for their guests, and Brenda quickly climbed the stairs to her apartment to get started.

Settled at her laptop, she brought up the name Logan Clark. It took almost twenty minutes for her to find anything about his life before he had become a successful textile broker. She dialed Mac.

"I found something interesting. Logan Clark went from rags to riches. He wandered around a lot until he met Jane. She was from a long line of wealthy people and her father finally resigned himself to her choice. He then pulled Logan into the family business of textiles and taught him everything he knows today, apparently."

"That's interesting," Mac said. "Bryce has discovered Logan never graduated from that college. In fact, he enrolled but never actually attended, so technically was never a student there. Did you find out his past addresses before he met Jane?"

"I'm still looking. I'll get back to you if I find anything."

Logan hurried to Sheffield Bed and Breakfast. He asked Allie if his wife was on the premises. Allie told him she had seen Jane go upstairs a short time before. He took two steps at a time and reached their room to find Jane taking clothing from shopping bags. She held up a shirt for him to admire.

"I bought this at a little boutique downtown. What do you think?"

When he didn't answer, Jane looked up and noted the wild look in his eyes. He went to the closet and began yanking his clothes from the hangers and then lifted his suitcase from the storage shelf. "We have to leave right away, Jane. I have an emergency in New York."

"I don't want to leave so soon, Logan. Tomorrow is Sunday. Can't it wait? I doubt your office will be open on the weekend anyway."

"We have to go right now, Jane." He continued to throw his clothing into the large suitcase and then snapped it shut. He retrieved his overnight case. "Hurry up. We have to get on the road."

Jane looked at her purchases. She was just getting into the life of the quaint village by the ocean. Every shop owner accepted her as if they had known her forever. Jane had a love for traveling and had spent time in Europe in high-class hotels both there and in America. Sweetfern Harbor was the first place she had ever visited where she felt completely at home. The experience was new to her and she yearned for more.

"You go ahead, Logan. I'm staying here until check-out time tomorrow." Her husband recognized the familiar determination signaling that his wife had made up her mind. "When you get the matter taken care of, call me." She smiled to herself. "In fact, I like the relaxed atmosphere around here so much that I may ask Brenda if I can stay the rest of the week."

Logan threw up his hands. "If that's the way you want it, Jane." He closed the last case and started for the door. She expected him to kiss her good-bye when he turned around. Instead, he opened his billfold and placed two credit cards on the table near the door. "Do you need cash?" he asked. She assured him she traveled prepared.

Logan didn't close the door completely behind him

and Jane saw him hesitate before choosing the back stairway to leave. He would have to walk around the building to the side parking lot where the guests parked. Jane shrugged and started making her own plans. Jenny Jones had asked her to have dinner with her before she left town. At the time, Jane told her they were leaving the next day. She had no qualms about returning downtown to ask if the invitation was still open to her. She went down to the front desk and asked Allie if the room she was in had been booked through Wednesday. Allie looked at her computer and told her not until the following weekend.

"Logan had to leave for an emergency and I would like to stick around a while longer. Your town fascinates me and everyone is so friendly. I can't leave just yet." Allie smiled and checked her in for another few days. She asked Jane her plans and was told she was on her way again to the shops. "I can't get enough of the specialty boutiques."

At first, Brenda heard footsteps on the back stairs and thought Mac came home early. She realized that was impossible because she had just talked with him. She shrugged it off, remembering the fact that guests were allowed to use the back stairs as well. Many times over the years one or more got up in the middle of the night to take advantage of the snack and beverage nook. Ignoring the fast footsteps on the stairs outside her apartment, she returned to her search about Logan Clark's history.

The man was elusive, she discovered. Brenda was ready to set it aside when she decided to look further into Bridgett and Thomas Mackey's lives. They were good neighbors and unassuming, though enjoyed their wealth. Bridgett showed interest in family history, according to some of her online posts, and for a short time Thomas' great-grandmother's pistol had been displayed behind glass at a local museum. They loaned it out for a month during Sweetfern Harbor History Month. Several gun collectors were interested in it but a newspaper article Brenda found quoted the woman as saying that she would never sell it, according to one potential buyer.

Buried in the narrative about the Mackey family history, one name surfaced. Brenda was stunned when she read the short sentence. "Logan Clark, handyman for the Mackey's, confirmed that Mrs. Mackey was adamant about preserving family heirlooms." Nothing else was said about the man, but Brenda didn't need anything else. She called Mac.

Mac gave a low whistle when he heard the news. "Someone educated in marketing doesn't usually end up working odd jobs. Tell Logan I want to see him again right away. There are enough discrepancies in his last statements to cause red flags."

Brenda walked down the hallway and knocked on the door of the room the Clarks occupied. When there was no answer, she went downstairs to ask her reservationist if she knew where they were.

"Logan had an emergency with his company in New York and left a little while ago. Jane stayed and is booked through this coming Wednesday. She went downtown."

Brenda went pale. Without answering Allie's questioning look, Brenda called Mac right away and told him what had happened. Mac ended the call quickly and summoned Bryce to get two cops to search for Logan Clark. He then alerted the Highway Patrol.

Brenda called Jenny, Molly and Hope to ask if Jane Clark was in any of their shops. No one had seen her yet. "If she does show up, give me a call, then try to keep her around until I get there. Act casual." None of them asked questions and promised to be on the lookout.

Jane sucked in the salty ocean air and took a good look at the quaint architecture along the streets of Sweetfern Harbor. She envisioned simplifying her lifestyle and moving there. It would be an ideal place to set up her design studio. Lost in her thoughts, she was startled when she heard her name called. Molly Lindsey waved to her from the door of the coffee shop and invited her in for a latte. It seemed to be Jane's choice the two times she had visited Morning Sun Coffee and Molly remembered it when she spotted the woman strolling down the sidewalk. Jane accepted. She knew she had the rest of the day to herself and vowed to spend it leisurely. Molly chatted with her for a couple of minutes and then went behind the counter to make the latte, but not before she called Brenda. When she came back with it, she smiled at Jane.

"I hope you don't mind if I take my break with you."

"I don't mind at all. Logan left for New York and I'd like some company." Molly poured herself a cup of coffee and joined her. Small talk flowed easily while she waited for Brenda to arrive. In a few minutes, the owner of the bed and breakfast walked in. She greeted Jane and Molly, and ordered a cup of lemon verbena tea. She asked Jane if she could join her.

"Of course," Jane said. "I don't know if you heard—my husband had some sort of an emergency in New York and left all of a sudden. Allie told me the room is mine through

Wednesday." She laughed softly. "In fact, she said it won't be booked again until next weekend. I'm getting attached to Sweetfern Harbor, much to my surprise, and I may stay until your next booking."

"We'd love to have you. Will Logan be back soon?"

She shook her head. "Who knows? I didn't even ask him this time what the emergency was. I can't imagine what would call him back on a weekend. Usually, problems can wait until Monday, but he insisted. He left in a hurry."

Brenda began to pave the way for an informative conversation. "I know what it's like to have a busy husband, mine works late all the time. Did I ever tell you how we met? At first I don't think he thought highly of me, though he adamantly denies that. Anyhow, we fell in love and in our mid-forties, we married. This is his second marriage. His first wife passed away ten years ago from an illness. Jenny's Blossoms is owned by my step-daughter."

Jane's expression marred by brief sadness. "You are lucky to have a daughter. I've never had children of my own and as far as I know neither has Logan. We met when I attended a textile convention to see what was out there. I don't design any fabric wares but I have to know some trends to coordinate my houseware designs. We married a few years ago. Most of my life has involved my career."

"What did Logan do before he got into the textile business?"

"He told me he worked for a landscaping company. My father was very much against the idea of me marrying someone he deemed penniless. He thought Logan was after my money. My father was wrong, Logan is a businessman. I persisted until my father gave in. He told me Logan had to promise to make something of himself or he would see that the marriage was dissolved." Jane laughed. "We were in our forties by then and I knew he was powerless to do anything. I have to give him credit for stubbornness, though. My father decided Logan's career for him and trained him to be a broker in the industry."

"Why was Logan at a textile convention if he didn't know anything about them at the time? I don't mean to pry, but I'm curious."

"He was there with a wealthy couple who were getting ready to redecorate their family home. He had driven a second vehicle along with them to bring the stuff back. Now that I think about it, I have no idea how the truck driving fit in with his landscaping. I didn't care, though. It was enough that he was handsome. He's always been so tan and well-built and charming. Something drew us to one another, even though we didn't date until much later."

Molly finished her cup of coffee and had to get back to the front counter, so she asked if they would like anything to eat. Brenda ordered iced tea and Jane asked for the same.

Brenda wanted to get to the meat of her visit with Jane Clark. "Will Logan call you when he gets into New York?"

"I'm sure he will. He's good about that. He'll tell me what the rush was about." The woman appeared completely relaxed. If her husband was involved in the cold case, she surely had no idea. Brenda realized Jane knew very little about her husband. His story about landscaping probably sounded better to her than admitting he had been a handyman when they first met. It was the disapproval of Jane's father's that was more telling, no matter how much Jane seemed to brush it off. As Brenda sipped her iced tea and chatted with Jane some more, she wondered what else Logan had managed to hide from his pretty yet oblivious wife over the years.

chapter six

Logan Clark loved Jane with all his heart. She was the first and only person he had ever loved. He felt disgusted that he couldn't tell her the real reason he had to escape Sweetfern Harbor. His life before meeting her had been like a bad dream, a terrible history he was pleased to leave behind him. The reality of what he had gone through and his actions would never be believed if he tried to tell the truth, so he did his best to forget.

Not everyone forgot, however. Annette Pickard had proved she knew Hal Pickard. It felt as if Logan looked directly into Hal's eyes when he looked closely at Annette. Other than that resemblance, she must have gotten her attractive looks from her mother. Who would have believed Hal would have a child who was into literary pursuits? It was about as far from Hal's life of crime as it could possibly be.

Driving down the highway, Logan jerked back to reality. He knew he must find a place to hide out for the next several days. He would call Jane before he left the interstate. If his calls were ever traced, he didn't want them to show up from somewhere that held no relevance to his life.

He took the exit to the rest area and parked. He called Jane to let her know he was almost home. "Why don't you stay there a few extra days, Jane? You seem to be enjoying yourself."

Jane told him she had already booked extra days and chatted with her husband about her lovely shopping excursion that morning and her chat with the owner of the bed and breakfast. Hal quickly got off the phone when he learned Brenda was right there; it was too close for comfort knowing that the detective's wife might be listening to their conversation.

As Jane chatted with her husband, Brenda held her breath. When Jane ended the call, Brenda asked innocently if he had arrived home safely. Jane told her he was almost there.

Knowing that Jane Clark wasn't going anywhere soon, Brenda excused herself and told her guest to enjoy the rest of the day. "I'll see you at dinner tonight."

On her way back to Sheffield Bed and Breakfast, Brenda called Jenny and Hope to tell them they didn't have to be on the alert any longer. She called Mac to tell him she thought Jane had no idea of anything amiss with Logan. She explained the conversation.

"They are definitely in love," she said. "She seems to have no idea that he might be hiding anything. Her innocence and their love may be what brought him back here."

"He may be innocent of any serious crime, Brenda, but

my gut feeling is he knows more than he's letting on. And I'm sure it has something to do with the Mackey murders."

Brenda couldn't argue with that. "If we can find out who he's protecting, that may explain why he's skirting around the truth of his background."

When she came into the foyer, Brenda had an idea. She asked Allie if Logan's signature was on file. Allie stated that he'd signed in when they arrived. Brenda looked over her shoulder at the signature on the screen. She asked Allie to print it off for her and then took it upstairs. Mac had decided to leave the handwritten note in their apartment when he took the chest and its items to the police station. She spread the letter open carefully and looked at the handwriting, examining the letters one by one. It seemed hopeless. Once again, she vowed to take classes in how to decipher and analyze handwriting. She put it all aside hoping Mac would see something she missed.

Everyone gathered in the dining room that evening for dinner, including Mac, who arrived home just in time. Brenda sensed he had something to tell her and they both excused themselves before dessert was served. Mac told her he had spent the rest of the afternoon looking at the records of a criminal who once hung around Sweetfern Harbor.

"I still haven't gotten to the end of reading the cold case. Quite a lot of work was done on the case and it's a thick folder. However, one name that caught my attention was Hal Pickard. He was someone the police suspected early on. They never gathered proof and so he wasn't charged with the crime." Brenda already knew this but she waited. "I looked into back files on Hal Pickard. He dabbled in petty crimes, mainly stealing. However, in one instance he got caught for attempted kidnapping. And this is the kicker, Brenda. A Logan Clark was a suspect as someone in on the crime with Mr. Pickard. They proved Pickard tried to take the bank teller along with the money she put together for him, and there was a driver of a car who might have been Logan, but there was no proof placing Logan anywhere near the scene of the crime."

"But Hal did get caught and was tried. Isn't that why he's in prison?"

Mac nodded. "Also, there was never any real proof a getaway car waited for him. He never admitted how he planned to escape after the burglary. The only thing that kept him from going to prison for life is the fact he didn't actually pick up the bag of money. The second security guard came in behind him in the middle of things and took over. They couldn't say he robbed the bank when he didn't walk out with the money, it was just attempted robbery and attempted kidnapping. He didn't even have time to put his hands on the money."

Mac told her Hal Pickard had lived in Sweetfern Harbor from 1978 until early 1983. He disappeared off the radar until the most recent crime that landed him in jail, where he presently resided. Mac didn't know why Logan Clark was suspected at all. Once they cleared him among others questioned, he was allowed to go free. The file was unclear about why Logan's name had surfaced in the investigation in the first place.

"I'm curious about Annette Pickard. Don't you think it's a little interesting that she shares a last name with

Hal?" Brenda asked. "I think she should be questioned now that you're opening the cold case. We may find something about her that never came up."

"This is some case, Brenda. I feel like we are in the beginning stages, but the fact that we have guests named Pickard and Logan Clark, may hurry things along." He told Brenda that Logan had not arrived home in New York and in fact had not been located yet. Brenda reminded him that Annette Pickard remained at Sheffield Bed and Breakfast. She glanced at her watch when they heard guests coming up to their rooms.

Brenda went into the hallway and saw Annette coming toward her room.

"Mac and I would like to talk with you for a few minutes, Annette." Annette looked at her closed door just a few steps away and back at Brenda. "It won't take long."

Mac went downstairs to Brenda's private office with his wife and their guest. Annette stood inside the door until Brenda told her to sit down. She decided to be blunt. The time for beating around the bush was long past.

"Do you know Hal Pickard?" she asked.

"What about him?"

"Do you know him?"

Annette's shoulders slumped. Her lips pinched into a thin line. "He's my father."

Mac scooted forward on the edge of the folding chair. "Do you know why he is in prison right now?"

"I heard he robbed a bank or something. We're estranged. What does this have to do with me?"

"Did you know he lived in Sweetfern Harbor during the time of the well-known Mackey murders?" Mac eyed her closely. Her face grew ashen. She didn't answer. "I'm not saying he had anything to do with the crime. I'm just asking if you are aware of that."

"I don't know about my father's life except things my mother tells me on occasion. There wasn't much love between the two of them."

"I understand your book is based on facts that you believe happened, though it will come out as fiction," Brenda said. "What is the subject matter of the book?"

Annette colored a little, realizing what Brenda was hinting at. "It is about a murder that took place in a small town. I've taken things my mother has said about crimes she knows of and I've interviewed some people to gather information. I am putting it all together into a fabricated story that I hope will sell well. I have editing lined up, so the book is practically done."

"Where does your mother live today?" Mac said.

"She lives about thirty miles from me in Scranton, Pennsylvania."

"I would love to read your book and give a review for you ahead of your sales," Brenda said with a small smile.

Annette's hands clenched into fists and her breath came in a subtle gasp. "I don't usually do that. My agent is very good at taking care of initial sales. If you will excuse me, I have a deadline and should get back to my work." They heard her quick, nervous footsteps in the hall and going back up the stairs to her room.

After the writer left, Mac chuckled. "Nice try, Brenda. Do you think she is writing facts she know to be true?" Brenda nodded her head vehemently.

"I think I'll ask Allie to talk to Annette more about her

book tomorrow. She isn't due to check out until three in the afternoon."

When they emerged from the office, Tim Sheffield walked into the foyer. The corners of Brenda's mouth almost reached her ears. "What are you all dressed up for, Dad?" she teased.

"I have a special date with Morgan tonight. I had hoped you'd let her go home early for once."

"I had no idea you two had anything planned or I would have told her to leave early already. Where are you going?"

Tim's eyes danced. He pressed his finger to his lips. "That's for the two of us to know. Tonight's a very special night. I'm going to take her home now so she can get ready."

"I want to hear everything no later than tomorrow morning, Dad."

She and Mac headed back to their apartment. Brenda told Mac she thought her father was finally going to propose to their chef. Mac chuckled and told her to give them some space. "Mark my words, Mac Rivers, tonight is the night. I wish Phyllis hadn't gone home yet. She could get it out of Morgan. It's my father who is the impenetrable rock." Mac laughed at his wife. He took her hand and warmth flooded through both of them.

Brenda and Mac awakened early the next morning. Mac planned to spend some time in his office on the cold case. Bryce's interest increased and Brenda and Jenny resigned themselves to not seeing either of them for the rest of their Sunday. Phyllis sat in the empty dining room sipping coffee.

"I didn't expect you in today, Phyllis. You and William need a day you can call your own."

Her head housekeeper waved her hand. "He and the archaeologist Mr. Bennett plan to spend their day in the musty archives at the museum, so I have the entire day to myself. Even though William told me he would be home by noon, I know better." Phyllis smiled. Brenda told her she was without Mac all day. She suggested the two of them pick up Jenny and all go down to Morning Sun Coffee.

"It's been a while since Jenny has had a break from her flower shop. And a while since the two of us have had a chance to catch up on the local gossip."

Allie was working that Sunday because she had an entrance exam for college to take on Tuesday. Since Sundays were more laid back, she expected to get some studying in. Brenda asked her in private to find out all she could about Annette's book, specifically any suspected facts that would be included. Allie preferred that challenge over studying for a college entrance test and agreed to do it.

When the women walked down to the flower shop, Jenny was delighted to get away for a while and left the shop in the capable hands of her assistant. "We've been swamped the last few days. The nice weather has brought everyone in to admire and buy flowers. I'll have to plan bouquets for the big business convention coming up, too."

When they walked past Sweet Treats, the drifting aroma of freshly baked goods drew all three inside. Hope greeted them warmly and pushed the tray toward them that held samples. She pointed out the new cheesecake petit fours that she came up with.

"I hope to get it right and add it to the business convention desserts," she said. All three proclaimed her success. Phyllis asked her if she could get away to join them at the coffee shop. "I'd like to, but David is picking me up in a little while. We're going to spend the day on the water."

Jenny felt a twinge of envy but quickly brushed it away. Hope Williams rarely took time away from her shop. Her treats were in high demand around town. Jenny told her to have a relaxing day and a few doors down, the women entered Molly's shop. Jane Clark sat with a familiar man and his wife.

"Hello, Andy," Brenda greeted the man when he looked up at them. "You and all the crew are doing a great job on our new cottage. I can't believe your progress."

Andy's wife Tracy greeted the women. "I'll have to come around and take a look," she said.

Molly approached and hugged her mother. "Where's William today?" Phyllis explained his mission for the day. Morning Sun Coffee had a few customers in it and Molly pushed another table close to the one Jane and the Shelton's were seated at. Molly immediately caught Brenda's attention when she spoke.

"I've been hearing rumors that the construction crew dug up an old chest," she said. "Was there buried treasure in it, Brenda? I want to hear the whole story."

Brenda told her Rich Turner had known there was something hard beneath the surface and how she and Mac dug it up by hand that evening. "There were a few things inside, but we don't know yet if anything is significant."

"I remember my husband talking about an old chest that was buried somewhere. I'll have to ask him the details when I see him again." Jane briefly explained to the others that he had returned to New York on urgent business.

This was one comment that Brenda wouldn't let hang. "Did he say how long ago?"

"I don't think so. It had something to do with his time before I met him. He's tight-lipped about his former life. I think he's still afraid of my father and his threats about staying steady in his career. Logan was a landscaper before we met and my father didn't think that was good enough." The others smiled, imagining a doting, wealthy father concerned about his daughter's choices in men.

"I wonder how Logan knew about a chest buried here. Did he ever live here in Sweetfern Harbor?" Phyllis asked.

"He lived in a small town somewhere, but again I'm not sure where." Jane leaned back and her face grew sober. "You know, I have a feeling I know very little about my husband before we met." She shook her head. "It doesn't matter. I know what he's like now and luckily we have a very happy marriage. He tends to wait on me hand and foot and I have to admit I like that."

Brenda grew restless. She wanted to join Mac at the police station. She was aware that DNA had been preserved and wanted to ask Mac to compare it to Hal Pickard's and possibly Logan Clark's DNA, if they had his on record. She had no idea which evidence box held the samples found at the crime scene, but Mac would. If not, it wouldn't take long to find it.

Brenda excused herself and stated she had to make a phone call. She stepped outside and called Mac.

"I've thought of that, Brenda, but we're still looking for that evidence. After all these years, it seems some of the evidence was separated or possibly simply lost. We'll search for it as soon as Bryce and I finish reading this long report."

When Brenda came back inside she apologized to Phyllis and Jenny. "I'm going down to the police station for a little while." Her two friends stood simultaneously and stated they would walk with her.

Out again into the sunshine, Jenny spoke first. "Whatever is going on, we want to be a part of it all." Phyllis agreed. Brenda told them the latest and why she wanted to get down there. Both women were adamant that they wished to help search for the missing evidence.

"I'll ask the chief for clearance for the two of you, too, and between us we should be able to locate any misplaced or scattered evidence."

Mac explained that Police Chief Bob Ingram took the day off with his family at the ocean. After giving the group stern warnings, he agreed all three could go to the evidence room and start their search. He handed them gloves and waited until they put them on before going into the large room.

"Are all of these unsolved cases?" Phyllis asked, staring at the metal shelves full of boxes.

"Some have been solved and are marked as such. Unfortunately, there are too many still waiting," Mac said.

The women decided their strategy and began looking for anything marked *Mackey 1982* on envelopes or boxes, and other boxes from that same year. Jenny now understood the police were looking for Logan Clark. With surprise, she mentioned that his wife seemed to be a very nice person. Brenda assured her that Jane wasn't involved as far as they knew. The storage room grew quiet except for the rustle of papers and movements of cardboard and the murmurs of the three women as they sifted and sorted through decades of old files in search of what they needed.

Logan Clark drove off the main roads onto a county highway. He drew nearer the forested areas and chose an abandoned logging road to give him time to think things through. The complications in his life made his head want to explode and he feared there was no way to keep both his lovely wife and his partner in crime happy.

There was something about Hal Pickard that drew him as a friend. He often thought the criminal got a kick out of drumming up petty crimes. Hal was faithful to Logan in that he managed to shield him from getting caught with any evidence. Logan was very good at assessing situations and then paving the way for Hal to take what he wanted without being seen. Several times Hal made mistakes but Logan was always given an escape route and he appreciated Hal's allegiance to him.

When Hal went into the Mackey home without telling Logan ahead of time, Logan felt the man made a mistake since he could be careless without planning well. He knew he had to reciprocate the loyalty.

The abandoned Queen Anne structure set at the edge of the city limits of Sweetfern Harbor had been an ideal place to hide what Logan carried. A few yards from the trees, next to the dilapidated summer cabin that looked like it would probably fall apart, he dug into the ground after a rain softened the earth and buried the treasures. The police were getting too close to Hal, and Logan took it upon himself to take the evidence from the shabby apartment Hal lived in. If he hadn't, Hal would become one of the lifers in prison. At first Hal was furious when he discovered someone had stolen his loot. Logan never told him what he had done to save him. He knew Hal would force him to dig the chest up and give the valuables back to him. He told himself he did it to save his friend.

Hal got over it eventually. He enjoyed returning to his game of outsmarting the cops, most of the time. That incident taught Logan a lot. For the first time, he realized how close he had come to being charged with a serious crime. The cops were getting desperate. They looked for anything at all to charge the two men for murder and robbery. One cop was overheard stating a crime like that had to have taken more than one person. Logan was the second person they focused on.

The night he buried the chest stuck in his mind day and night for years. Once he came to know and love Jane, he almost spilled the beans to her. When he told her he knew of a buried chest somewhere that held valuables, he felt relief that she wasn't as interested in the subject as he thought she would be, and he dropped it. He supposed that if one grew up with wealth, a chest of valuables didn't mean as much. After that, he watched himself and never mentioned it again. She never asked him about it, either.

Annette Pickard came to his mind as he sat there on the abandoned logging road. Several had talked about the book she was writing after she left the sitting room one night at the bed and breakfast. The reservationist served them drinks and casually mentioned Annette told her the book was based on some facts but written as fiction. "An old crime," the young girl had said with excitement, "with just a few things changed to make it fiction." The very mention of it made Logan's stomach drop like a stone.

When Jane innocently asked the theme of the book, Allie told her she understood it was about a murder. Sick to his stomach, Logan then decided to find out if Annette was related to Hal. Was this a threat from his longtime partner? Was Annette going to expose them? He hoped to find a time when she wasn't in the bed and breakfast so he could steal the manuscript to read it. As it turned out, Annette Pickard rarely left her room except to go downstairs to eat.

When the cops had come asking about Logan's questions of Annette, he had followed his instincts and run, telling Jane some story about having urgent business in New York. What he truly needed was time to think and plan, and figure out exactly how to deal with the problem of Annette Pickard.

chapter seven

The police were coming up empty-handed in their search for Logan Clark. His wife had not heard from him and she was worried something terrible had prevented him from arriving home as planned. She regretted she hadn't asked him more about the sudden business emergency. Perhaps it was connected to his failure to contact her again. She repeated her concerns to Detective Rivers, and later with Brenda when alone in the bed and breakfast.

"I'm really worried, Brenda. It's not like him to not contact me. I know the police are looking for him and my greatest hope is that they will find him. Perhaps he's simply so tied up with work that he hasn't answered the phone, or had to drive to a meeting somewhere with no cell service."

Brenda bit her tongue to hold back the real explanation as to why the cops were searching for her husband. Instead, she reassured her guest that things would end well. She asked Jane about her design business and tried to divert attention from her worries.

"My chef complains about an over-abundance of pots and pans in the kitchen. I think you could give us some good pointers on how to be more efficient. She boxed up and stored some of them, but still feels the kitchen is inefficient."

"I'd be happy to take a look. Even in smaller home kitchens, most of us supply the cabinets with more than we actually need."

Brenda told her she would introduce her to Morgan when the chef was between meal preparations. "Whatever the two of you come up with is fine with me. We would be happy to have your design and organization help."

Jane was happy for the distraction. If she successfully reorganized the Sheffield Bed and Breakfast kitchen she could use the project as a future reference in Sweetfern Harbor. When she met Morgan, the chef happily accepted her help. Jane got to work daydreaming idly about relocating her entire business to the little seaside town, and tried not to think about what her husband would say about the idea.

Annette Pickard glanced at her watch as she listened to her mother on the phone at her ear. Four hours remained before time to check out. She grew weary of her mother's phone calls. The day would arrive when Mattie Pickard, or whoever's last name she now had, would get the shock of her life. Annette ended the call, set her phone on silent and bent to her work. Once she checked out of the bed and breakfast she had one important trip to take before returning to Pennsylvania. Annette decided to take her mother's endless calls after she got home, to prevent her from visiting in person. If everything worked out, and she expected positive results, then she would enjoy a new lifestyle someplace far away. Her meddling and complaining mother would be out of her life forever.

Allie smiled at the author when she came downstairs for her last lunch at the bed and breakfast. "How is your book coming along? I hope you've had the peace and quiet you hoped for."

"It has served me well," Annette said. "I wonder if I could take a box lunch to my room today. It may be too late to order that, but it sure would save me some time."

"Of course. I'll tell Anna right away and bring it up to you." Allie got her choices and Annette answered and thanked her.

Back in the room, Annette paced slowly back and forth. She stopped at the window that overlooked the new construction. At first, she had paid little attention to the conversation that flowed around the dinner table in the evenings. Then it had been mentioned that something had been brought up from the ground where the cottage was under construction. Later, she heard it was a small metal chest that may have held valuables of some sort. After that, Logan Clark began prying into her private business. Much later it dawned on her that his name was very familiar to her, but she didn't let on to him what she recalled. It was safer to ignore him. The day she reported him to Brenda Rivers was the day she felt she was done with his harassment. She shivered even now thinking how vulnerable she made herself the morning he followed her to the beach. Her relief when the housekeeper and her husband appeared made her very thankful for their intervention. Now, as she thought about escaping from this little town, she thought about how unprepared everyone would be for what would soon come out in her book. It gave her a strange feeling of pride, power and safety. After all, no one would know it was real.

When Brenda dug deeper into the cardboard box in the cold case room, she felt a dusty legal envelope at the very bottom and pulled it out. Only the date *1982* was written on it. She waved it to Phyllis and Jenny. The three looked inside and saw fingerprint records of Hal Pickard and a separate sheet for Logan Clark. A separate sheet recorded blood results for both men. Back in the eighties it was too early for DNA evidence, but it was one more clue that they might be able to use.

They went up to Mac's office and Brenda laid it on his desk triumphantly. "Where did you find this?" he said, looking up.

"It was in a separate box an aisle over from the larger one that has the Mackey name on it. For some reason it was by itself and stuck in the bottom of the bin." Brenda smiled at him. "We opened it and found the information you've been hoping for."

Mac and Bryce had admiration in their eyes, but only briefly. The fingerprints were a serious development. "We'll have to arrest Logan Clark when we find him," Bryce said. Mac cautioned him to make sure everything matched and proceed from there. Bryce hurried to the next room, where the recent findings were kept. Jenny followed him. The others waited until the young detective returned.

"We have fingerprint matches on the objects in the chest. Both Hal Pickard's and Logan Clark's fingerprints match."

"It proves Logan was in on the crime with Hal," Brenda said.

"It proves he handled the objects, but nothing from the crime scene indicates he was there at the time of the killings," Mac corrected her.

The two bantered back and forth about the details and Brenda realized if Logan's DNA was found in the Mackey house it wouldn't be unusual since he worked inside the home at times. "Are you sure he didn't leave evidence at the crime scene?"

Mac shook his head. "I've looked over it all with a fine-toothed comb and nothing at the scene indicated he was there."

Thoughts and possibilities raced through everyone's mind as they all sat in silence for a few minutes. "The crimes took place in the upstairs sitting room. There was no evidence showing Logan was on the second floor at any time," Bryce said. "His inside work was concentrated mainly around the kitchen area."

"Then how did his prints get on the artifacts from the chest?" Phyllis asked.

"I think he handled them later, after the crime was committed. I also feel sure he was the one who left the note in the chest," Brenda said. "We should have the answer back from the handwriting expert by tomorrow morning. I don't think he really thought anyone would find the buried chest in his lifetime."

"I don't understand why they buried it all," Jenny said. "Why not pawn it off for money?"

"Sweetfern Harbor is a small town and it would be hard to get by with that. They may have buried it with the intent to dig it up again at a later date." Mac rubbed his chin. "After the case had gone cold I think their intent was to take the valuables somewhere far from here and turn them in for cash. The fact is that Hal Pickard continued his crime spree and he ended up in jail again and again. Logan Clark appears to have disappeared from the radar after the murders."

"That must have been when he met Jane and turned his life around," Phyllis said. All agreed they had worked out the strongest scenario to date.

Mac pointed out that the fugitive crossed state lines when he checked into Sheffield Bed and Breakfast and then departed again for New York. Bringing in the FBI proved relevant now. Every agency in the Eastern United States was on alert. Yet Logan Clark evaded them all.

Logan was a thinker. He knew he had to gather supplies to last a while before every law agency emerged on his trail. He turned around and went back to the small gas station and store that sold everything a hiker or hunter would need. He paid in cash and then left. He drove rugged roads further into the mountains. In the next two hours he passed a couple who hiked a trail in the distance. He had to go deeper in. When he came to a small clearing he parked, hidden in the trees, and looked around him. The binoculars he kept in the glove compartment came in handy for the first time since Jane gave them to him three years earlier. He moved them slowly around the entire perimeter of the clearing. Only a few small animals scurried nearby.

The remnants of a burned-out campfire remained in the middle of the meadow. He had no intentions of starting a fire for any reason. Everything he brought could be eaten without the necessity of cooking. He wished he had his revolver but had given that up long ago when he turned from petty crimes to a better life. The only weapon available to him now was the short thick tree branch that fit snugly in his vehicle. By nightfall he curled up in the backseat and tried to think if there was any way out of the mess he currently found himself in. He would never survive long by living a rugged life. He began to wish he had kept driving along state and county roads. Canada wasn't that far away and if he left first thing in the morning he might avoid the law if any were looking for him. Something in the face of Detective Rivers told him he knew he had a connection with the Mackey murders. He had no doubt that when they discovered he had suddenly left the bed and breakfast the hunt for him would be on.

Logan counted on Jane to continue to believe in him.

Allie Williams waited for the chef to box up Annette's lunch. Morgan hummed softly with a secret smile on her lips and Allie became curious.

"Why are you so happy today, Anna?"

A pink tint crept into her face. "It's the last lunch for most of the guests until the next run."

"Ha," Allie said. "There's something else going on with you. What's the big secret?"

The chef shrugged her shoulders and hurried to complete the lunch. "This is ready for Miss Pickard when you are."

"Uh huh," Allie said with a grin. She vowed to get to

the bottom of things before her shift at the front desk was finished. Right now she had to take care of Brenda's request. She knocked on the writer's door.

Annette took the box and cold drink then thanked Allie. She started to close the door when Allie stopped her with her words.

"I know you have a lot of work to get done before you leave, Miss Annette, but this book of yours has really piqued my imagination. Do you have any excerpts I could read?"

"Not really," Annette said. "I'll have to allow my publisher to go through it, as usual. It should be out on the shelves in a month or less. Sorry, I have to get back to it."

Her tone of voice left no room for more inquiries. Allie had no choice other than to leave her to her tasks. When Brenda came into the front foyer, Allie told her of her failed attempt to get anything out of Annette regarding the novel. "I understand, Allie. She is definitely closed-mouthed about it. I suppose if she told too much about its contents no one would buy the finished piece." Brenda was not so sure that was Annette's motivation for secrecy, however.

"And by the way, Brenda, Chef Morgan is unusually happy today. She was even humming in the kitchen."

Brenda's eyebrows shot up. "That is unusual for her. I don't think I've ever heard her singing voice. Did you ask her why she was so happy?" Allie confirmed that she had but received only a brush off from the older woman. Brenda's smile widened. "I'm going to make a call to my dad and invite him over for dinner. I'll get something out of him yet."

"Do you think Morgan's so happy because he finally proposed to her?" Allie's eyes danced.

"I have a strong feeling something went on last night. They had a big date and he was dressed to the nines. If I can't get it out of him, I'm sure Phyllis will manage."

"Let me know what you find out. I'm very curious. If he did ask her to marry him, we have celebrations to plan." Allie's mind ran away with artistic decorating ideas for an engagement party and wedding.

"If they got married, he wouldn't have to sneak in visits through the back door with her," Brenda said. Both women laughed. "I don't know why he doesn't just come through the front entrance when he wants to see her."

Tim Sheffield's step was lighter that day. The woman he had come to love had said yes to his proposal. He agreed with Morgan to wait to announce the event. They wanted to enjoy the moment a while longer before his daughter and friends started going overboard with party planning. When Brenda's mother had passed away, he'd never thought about finding a new love. After all of these years, Morgan had come into his life in an unexpected way. Tim had reluctantly visited his daughter when she had inherited the bed and breakfast from his brother. He had hoped to sway her to return to her hometown and to her career that held promise. Running a small hotel wasn't something he approved of at first. But the more he observed Brenda at work, the more he realized she was truly happy for the first time in a long while.

He sold his home in Michigan and moved to Sweetfern Harbor at her urging. He believed it had been in the cards all along to make that decision. If he hadn't, he would have remained morose and sad, living his life alone, and he never would have met the beautiful, kind Morgan, whose companionship he had grown to treasure.

At ten minutes before three that afternoon, Annette Pickard descended the staircase. Allie called the porter, who retrieved her bags at the top of the stairs. She carried a briefcase and her laptop. Allie asked her if she had enjoyed her stay, and Annette told her it was just what she had needed. While the reservationist entered data into the computer, Jane Clark appeared in the hallway.

"I'm meeting again with your chef. Is it all right if I go on down to the kitchen?" Allie assured her it was fine.

Annette watched the woman turn and then asked if Mr. Clark had left.

"My husband left a couple of days ago. He had an emergency at work."

"I understand your home is in New York," Annette said. "Have you always lived there?"

Jane hesitated, as if wondering why she was receiving questions from someone who had rarely spoken to anyone else during her stay. "I'm from there. Logan and I have lived there since our marriage."

Annette started to ask something else, but retreated to her usual quiet demeanor and accepted the final printout from Allie. Jane continued to the kitchen.

"I suppose the Clarks are wealthy people," Annette remarked. "New York is not a cheap place to live."

"I guess so," Allie said. "Jane decided to stay a few days longer to help organize the kitchen here. She is a designer in housewares."

Annette thanked Allie for a pleasant stay. She met

Brenda, who came from the sitting room and thanked her as well. Brenda told her to come back any time and wished her success with her novel.

When the door closed behind her, Allie shook her head. "Something is strange about that woman. I don't know what it is, but there definitely something about her that is mysterious."

"Maybe all writers are like that," Brenda said. "I don't think she is strange, perhaps it's just a quirk of her personality. She isn't one to interact well with other people. Perhaps that explains why she is a successful writer. She immerses her talents into her characters and narratives rather than real people."

On the back roads, Logan Clark returned to a secondary roadway that headed north. When nightfall approached, he searched for lodging off the beaten path, some place that would accept cash and wouldn't ask too many questions. The run-down roadside Mystic Inn caught his eye. It wouldn't be his first choice in his usual world, but his normal lifestyle didn't apply now. The tall lanky man behind the desk was happy to accept his cash.

The twenty-something clerk had seen all kinds of people check into the seedy motel, even those who looked like they could afford better accommodations. They wanted one thing only and there were plenty of people hanging around in the bars around this rural area to serve them. He took the cash and handed Logan the key to Room 23, out back of the structure. Logan intended to give a fake name, but none was requested.

The only plus of the room was the clean sheets on the bed. He threw them all the way back. There were no uninvited varmints hiding between the linens. The dim exposed lightbulb in the bathroom hid the place's imperfections well and he kept his shoes on.

He must look for better lodgings from here on out. He also had to think about how he would safely drive into Canada at the checkpoint. He had his passport with him, but worried if the law was looking for him, all borders would be on alert for Logan Clark.

Since going on the run, nightmares had invaded his dreams. The sights and sounds of that night returned to him and the bloody bodies of Bridgett and Thomas Mackey showed up during the nighttime. He was safe from that event and Hal was in prison on another charge. There was no proof he had any connection with that crime. His sole intent had been to protect his friend and he had done that. Yet the nightmares dogged him and he feared he had a long way to go before he could truly escape the consequences of his friendship with Hal Pickard.

chapter eight

nnette headed to upstate New York. She picked up a newspaper at the convenience store and in her car she read the latest story in the headlines. Word had gotten out about a mysterious metal chest found buried in the backyard of historic Sheffield Bed and Breakfast. Daughters of a couple slain in Sweetfern Harbor back in 1982 came forward and identified the objects as heirlooms their parents once had in their home. The story described the gruesome murders and robbery. The objects had never surfaced and no one knew where they had been until a contractor discovered something in the ground behind the establishment. The owners became curious and dug it up. Detective Mac Rivers and his wife Brenda Sheffield Rivers then delved into the cold case that surrounded the murders.

Two suspects had never been apprehended because of lack of evidence. Annette read her father's name as the most prominent suspect, and that of Logan Clark as his accomplice. A small smile touched her lips. Everything fit with the details her mother had told her over the years and now new details came back to Annette. Her mind raced. She knew things about her father's petty crime sprees and the attempted kidnapping of a bank teller, though she doubted he would stoop to murder.

Annette added that to her list and pulled into the parking lot for visitors at the state prison.

Hal Pickard was notified he had a visitor. The guard walked with him to the visiting room. When he saw the attractive young woman in front of him, he stopped for a moment. He had never imagined such beauty. Thoughts of a younger Mattie came back to him. He didn't have to think of how his daughter's voice sounded. They had often spoken on the phone over the years, including during his various stints in prison. He had cautioned her every time never to visit him, so it was a shock to see her here, and it worried him.

"You don't need to be associated with me other than through phone calls, Annette." He always reminded her of that before the calls ended. He remembered his own words as he sat down across from her, waiting to hear what she had to say.

Over the years they had developed codes in their communications. Hal gave her advice on the supposed pet dog she owned, referring to it as Azul. Annette put two and two together about the intended phrasings during the second call after the murders in 1982. She knew he referred to his partner of the past. When he spoke of Azul 'hiding bones,' she was smart enough to know he suspected his partner of stealing the loot he had taken from the Mackey home. The problem was she had no idea who Azul really was until she met Logan Clark and he started asking suspicious questions. Today was the first time she had seen her father face to face since she was a child. His hair was cut neatly and a lot of grey strands stood out. He had a slight stoop to his shoulders. She wanted to hug him but knew that was against the rules. They sat across from one another and Hal's broad yet nervous grin wouldn't stop.

After a short chit-chat, she condensed the story of her recent stay at Sheffield Bed and Breakfast. "I met Logan Clark, who was there with his wife," she said.

Hal gasped and leaned back. "Are you sure it was him?"

"I'm sure. He is a wealthy man now. But there is more."

Hall hung on to her every word. The buried metal chest demanded more detail. Annette told him of the article in the recent newspaper. "You wondered who stole your valuables from the Mackey home. It was Azul, a.k.a. Logan Clark. That's who you've been referring to in our phone calls all these years, isn't it?" Hal nodded. "I'm sure he's the one who buried the chest there when the property was abandoned. At first I thought he did it hoping to sell the items, and that was how he got his wealth. But if that was his motive, why did he bury it?"

A slight smile flashed on Hal's face. "We always had one another's backs. Maybe he was afraid I'd get caught with the valuables and it would point to me as the murderer." Annette didn't want to find the real truth yet. She skipped over that possibility. Hal read her mind. "Someday you'll know the whole truth, Annette, but not necessarily at this point. Just know that I stole the things from the Mackey's, but it was on a different day than their murders."

"I have researched quite a bit for the next book I'm writing," Annette said. "It will be fiction but there is something in the findings you may not know about." She paused to reflect on his facial expression. It had not changed but his hands were clasped tighter together. "Mother was having an ongoing affair with Logan Clark while you were married to her. She was with Logan when he took the items from your apartment. She has rattled on against you enough over the years, and, listening to her, it didn't take much to connect the dots. She likes to drink. In one of her stupors she admitted the affair. She belabored the point that she should be married to him today for his wealth."

This time Hal's face changed and anger flared in his eyes. "You know what has to be done now, don't you?" Annette nodded her head. A sudden thought made him crease his brow. "Wait a minute—are you the author that Mattie told me was writing my life story?"

"I'm writing a novel, but it's not a biography about you. Your name isn't mentioned in it, though my mother's shows up quite often. She's no angel and often over the years has managed to poison your name every chance she gets. I think that when it is ready for the presses, my revenge against her will come to light and all will see the true Mattie. Logan Clark will lose his status in the textile broker business."

"Annette, I did not kill Bridgett and Thomas Mackey."

She ignored the watching guards and reached for her father's hand. "I know you didn't, Dad."

It had been many years since Hal Pickard felt he had a true ally. His daughter was smart. Annette kept her life above board and wasn't on anyone's radar other than as an author. He recalled his many antics with Logan Clark. He realized the man managed to stay on the outside of every crime. Hal did have to thank him for setting everything up for perfect heists, but Logan was never found to be a part of any crime except in low level instances. None merited prison. He seethed when he remembered Mattie's beauty and Logan's youthful good looks. His partner was as adept at keeping the affair secret as he was evading crimes in action.

"Annette, I want to ask one more thing of you."

"For you, Dad, anything."

"Keep in touch with your mother, even though I know she's a tiresome woman. We need to get more out of her. She likes to drink. Wait until she's tipsy and find out all you can from her."

Annette promised him she would do anything, and this was no exception. It was worth it to put up with Mattie a while longer. They promised one another to continue with their codes and added a new one. In place of Mattie, they would refer only to Sadie, who would be added as a second pet of Annette's.

On her way home to Pennsylvania, Annette bought a bottle of Kentucky Bourbon.

Brenda sat down at her laptop. Something nagged at her about Logan Clark. He married into a wealthy family and from all appearances left his life of petty crime behind him. She thought about Jane's remark about not knowing her husband as well as could be expected. Logan had never been in prison, so transitioning to an upright life may not have been that hard for him. She read from his history that he was a natural when it came to applying business sense to new expertise in textiles.

There wasn't much more to learn about Logan Clark. Brenda switched to Annette Pickard. Her birthplace of Scranton, Pennsylvania was mentioned. Her mother was listed as the parent and her name was Mattie Pickard. Brenda surmised that Mattie was a single mother. The early childhood of Annette held little detail, but she earned a degree in journalism. She worked at a newspaper office for several years and then stopped to begin writing novels.

Brenda was impressed with her success. Her publisher recently announced another upcoming book about a crime in a small town. The press release stated some of it was based on facts of a real life crime, but Annette had woven the story as fictional. This novel would prove to be her most triumphant publication yet, the article said. By now, Brenda's interest in the novel grew deeper with suspicion. Her gut feeling told her Annette may reveal something about a cold case, but could it be the one in Sweetfern Harbor long ago? Brenda tried not to get her hopes too high. It was a long shot.

She felt rather than saw Mac's presence and turned around in time to receive a kiss from him. "What are you up to, Brenda?"

"I hoped to find out more about Annette Pickard. I'm also more than a little curious about this book she's been working on. I can't wait to read it."

When Mac questioned her, she explained her strong

feelings about Annette's proposed fictional novel. "I think she knows something about Mackey murders we're working on. She did admit Hal Pickard was her father and I'm not sure she told the truth about being estranged from him. She tried to convince us he was of little interest to her."

Mac didn't follow what his wife said. "I don't see how her book could possibly connect with the crime. She wasn't even been born then. What could she know that would cause her to write it into a novel?"

"She was raised by her single mother. Maybe her mother was a witness and told her about it or something."

"That's possible," Mac said. The familiar response of running his hand through his hair told her he was trying to follow her logic.

"I told Morgan to fix our dinner as carry-out. I thought we could eat up here and then go take a look at the progress on our cottage. Most of the guests have left except for Jane. Morgan and her helpers will join her in the dining room, and my father is also eating here tonight."

"That's a good idea, Brenda. I'm ready for some private time together."

Meanwhile, Jane Clark had become even more concerned about her husband. She had not heard from him since the call saying he was almost home. She hesitated to call her father about the matter but was aware she couldn't put that off much longer. He expected Logan back at work by Tuesday morning. She took a walk around the grounds to think things through. There was nothing in his demeanor to cause her to wonder about him. She recalled he clearly didn't want her to go down to the ocean the morning he went on his own. He told her that he had to think some things out in regard to a business matter. Her father was usually on top of everything. She breathed a little easier knowing he must know what was going on with Logan and the work problem. Maybe they are at a meeting together, she thought. That did not waylay her concerns. It was unlike Logan not to call her daily when they were apart.

Jane met Brenda as she went into the dining room. Brenda walked toward the kitchen to pick up the food. "Have you heard from Logan yet?" Brenda asked.

"No, and I've been thinking about him a lot. He hasn't called me at all. I'm going to call my father after dinner. They may be together and immersed in whatever the problem was that had to be taken care of." Her face grew taut. "It's so unusual that he hasn't called. When we are apart, he always calls at least once each day and usually more."

"I'm sure you will be hearing from him soon. Let us know if there is anything we can do."

Jane thanked her. In the dining room she was introduced to Brenda's father, Tim Sheffield. She had been helping Morgan organize her kitchen and had met the two servers who joined them, too. She smiled to herself when she saw the looks exchanged between Tim and Morgan. The conversations flowed easily between all of them. Tim spoke of the bed and breakfast that his brother restored after purchasing it.

"It had been abandoned for several years and was in bad shape," Tim said. "Randolph told me that there was an enormous amount of trash on the grounds in back. It seems the young people around town took advantage and threw parties out there."

"And Brenda and Mac found that buried chest," Morgan said. "I don't think anything of value was in it since she hasn't said anything else about it."

"If Randolph had known it was out there he would have dug it up," Tim said. He laughed at the memories of his brother. "He was into collecting artifacts found here."

Jane repeated the brief statement her husband had made regarding an old chest buried someplace. "I have no idea where it is. I should have paid more attention. Now I'm curious about what he was talking about, but he never brought it up again."

"Whatever he meant, it must have been important to him," Morgan said.

"That's why I've thought more about it since Brenda and Mac found this one. I never knew Logan was interested in old things at all. I wish he had been free to stick around here a few more days with me, but I'll ask him when I get home."

Brenda and Mac finished their meal. They took a stroll along the waters and then found their favorite spot again in the backyard. They were both impressed with the progress on their home. Brenda couldn't help but talk of the unsolved case. "I think Annette Pickard should be called back for more questioning," she said.

"What kind of questions?"

Brenda shook her head. "I really don't have anything specific. I wonder when that book of hers is coming out."

Mac laughed. "I know you are counting on that book to give us answers, Brenda, but I just don't see it."

"Something tells me we'll learn facts from it." Mac was intrigued by Brenda's insistence, though he reserved judgment. Brenda often proved right, however. They talked for long hours, poring over the nuances of the case.

Annette Pickard was home again. So far her mother had not called, though this didn't surprise her much. Mattie didn't know when she had planned to return. When she did call the next morning, Annette could tell she had already begun imbibing for the day. Her words were slurred together somewhat, but she kept the conversation thread going better than her daughter expected.

"I think I'll stop and see you later today, Annette."

Annette frowned. After being away for several days, Mattie couldn't even bring herself to ask how her trip was. "I've been out of town, Mother. Do you even remember that?"

Mattie pushed off her questions and claimed she was perfectly sober, though Annette could hear the plain truth in her voice.

"I'm interested in hearing more about Hal," Annette said. Mattie started to protest. "Come on over. I brought you something you'll like." Twenty minutes later, Mattie appeared at her door. Annette showed her the bourbon and asked her if she wanted to try it. Mattie was happy to do so.

"I thought about the affair you and that Logan Clark had together. I don't blame you for it, especially if your marriage wasn't a happy one."

Mattie took a long drink from the cocktail glass and Annette refilled her drink. "Logan Clark was the most handsome man you'd ever want to meet. We were a team.

I divorced your father because I thought Logan and I would get married. I helped him in a crime or two and believed he'd be grateful." She took another drink. "He just used me and after the last big one he just disappeared." Mattie attempted to snap her fingers but failed.

"What do you mean the last big one? Are you talking about the last big theft?" Annette stood to retrieve the bottle and refilled Mattie's glass again.

"It was big all right." The chortle that followed came from deep in her throat. "Logan was smart. I have to give him that much. Your father wasn't so smart. He was like a puppet in Logan's hands." She held out her glass and Annette poured a half glass. Mattie didn't notice the amount and part of it sloshed out as she brought it to her mouth, ranting about her memories and past glories.

While Mattie rambled, Annette took it all in and allowed the information to set in her mind as if in stone. Her heart had hardened too, and she knew her father was right. She knew what she had to do.

chapter nine

Another two weeks passed and Logan Clark was still on the run. Jane was back home and notified Brenda that no one knew where he was. They had hired private investigators to look for him, to no avail. Detective Mac Rivers continued to come up dry, as did the rest of the force.

It was Allie who waved a book in her face after breakfast one morning.

"The book you've been waiting for is out, Brenda," she said.

Brenda snatched it from her without apology, surprised that she had forgotten about it in the search for Logan Clark. She flipped through the table of contents first. The chapter heading that caught her eye was *The Truth About Azul*, followed by one called *The Real Sadie*. Brenda took the book into her office and sat down to skim through the details. The first chapter started with the gruesome murder of a respected couple in a town named Harbor Village. The couple was described as guardians of family histories and the type who contributed generously to the upkeep of historic sites. The author did not speak of their wealth but it was easy to read between the lines.

Phyllis stuck her head in the doorway and started to ask Brenda a question. Brenda held up her hand signaling she was otherwise engrossed. Phyllis backed out and she and Allie looked at one another.

"She's really into that book," Allie said. "I wonder what has her so captivated." Phyllis asked her what the book was about and when the reservationist told her, she nodded her head knowingly.

"That's the one she is sure will help solve the cold case she and Mac are working on."

"Are you saying Annette Pickard may have written a true story?"

"I don't know for sure," Phyllis said, "but I do know that Brenda feels strongly it holds some vital information. Let's leave her alone to find what she needs and then we'll get her to tell us."

The two employees were confident their boss and friend would have plenty to say. Phyllis crossed her fingers hoping the answers were there. Brenda had the ability to read and absorb content faster than anyone Phyllis knew. Lunch time arrived and Brenda read on. Allie asked Phyllis if she should take a tray to her. They agreed it was a good idea and when Allie brought it into the office, Brenda glanced up and thanked her before returning to the novel.

Brenda nibbled on the watercress sandwich and chips. Finally, she stood up and stretched. When she emerged Phyllis came from the sitting room where she had been tidying up. Allie turned expectant eyes from her computer.

"I'm going to take a long walk down by the ocean," Brenda said. "I feel the need for some fresh salty air."

Phyllis had no intentions of letting her off that easily. "We've been waiting all day for you to finish that book, Brenda. Tell us something at least. You can't keep us in suspense like this."

Brenda chuckled. "I did find some things I feel certain describe how things unfolded back in 1982. She doesn't give the year but the details mesh too closely with what the police know. She has to have inside information. I have to think things out and then call Mac. I promise I will tell you when I know more."

That was all they were going to get for now. Brenda didn't go down the rocky path to the waters. She chose to sit on the lower end of the wall that separated Sheffield Bed and Breakfast from the drop below. She listened to the ever-faithful waves lapping below her and thought about Annette's writings. Brenda and Mac had read and reread the entire findings on the case to date. The author not only spelled out those discoveries but had also answered questions about the case that could tie up all the loose ends.

There was no mistaking that the character Azul matched a former guest of hers who was now on the run. As for 'Sadie,' Brenda decided there was an unknown in the cold case that no one had thought existed. She called Mac.

"I finished the latest novel Annette Pickard just

published. I have to talk with you right away. Is Chief Ingram in today?"

"He's right here in my office. I'll call Bryce in, too. Come on down, we'll all chat together."

When Brenda arrived at the police station, she walked in with the novel in her hand.

"Logan Clark must be found as soon as possible," she said. "He is the most important person involved in this case, and this book proves why." She continued to explain the writings. "Hal Pickard stole those valuables the day before the murders. The Mackey's were out for the evening at the local museum. It was displaying rare artifacts, some of which were traced back to the Mackey family. Logan was a handyman back then who had developed quite a friendship with Bridgett and Thomas Mackey. Bridgett was eager to talk about the history of her husband's family tree. Logan paved the way for Hal Pickard to enter and rob them. Hal and Logan had a pact —they would divide the items one day and equally share in the money they brought in. However, Hal jumped the gun and broke in the day before, without Logan's knowledge."

"Brenda, I thought this novel was fiction," Mac said.

"It is published as fiction, but too many facts we already know are spelled out. How else could Annette Pickard know some of these things? There are some things that only this department is aware of, other than the perpetrators. I don't know how Annette gathered so much information, but she hit the nail right on the head."

The Chief encouraged her to continue.

"The biggest mystery is the character Sadie. I can't

figure out exactly who she is but I do know she and Logan, a.k.a. Azul, were having an affair. She knew everything that transpired. I know Logan is married to Jane now, but I don't believe they knew one another until he turned his life around. There must be someone else."

Detective Bryce Jones spoke up. "I spent a lot of time researching Jane. I didn't find anything that told me she did anything against the law. That is, if we're not counting the life she led while in college. She was a bit wild then, but nothing criminal in her background."

The knock on Mac's door interrupted them. "We got him, Detective Rivers," the young officer said. He handed Mac the notice that Logan Clark had been apprehended in Newfoundland. "He made it into Canada without getting caught. Seems he was staying in a hotel there. All hotels throughout Canada had been notified to be on the lookout. When the notice came in, the manager looked over the roster of guests and apparently Logan used his real name. It was the manager who engaged him in a conversation, then called the local police right after that." The officer told the group their fugitive was on his way back to the United States.

"I think Logan Clark will tell us who this Sadie is," Bob said. The chief congratulated everyone, telling them their persistence finally paid off.

After the chief left, Brenda asked Mac what his thoughts were on how Annette had gotten so much information. "She maintains Hal stole the items the day before the murders. The Mackey's hadn't missed them until the next day when Bridgett looked into their safe to find a document they were going to donate to the museum. That was also the day they were murdered."

"Logan Clark wanted more," Mac said. "I think he was greedy and had already weaseled his way into the Mackey's lives. I think Bridgett showed him more items of value and he wanted them for himself."

"Annette writes that 'Sadie' was introduced to the Mackey's that fateful morning," Brenda said. "Apparently, Bridgett trusted Logan enough to not fear Sadie's knowledge of the items. It was Logan who later went to Hal's apartment when he wasn't home. He took the items Hal stole and supposedly buried them on our grounds to protect Hal from the law." Brenda explained the complicated story Logan had concocted, and how the book hid the real facts in plain sight.

"After all these years, we know Hal Pickard is no murderer," Bryce said. "Logan must have returned for more and murdered the couple in the process. I wonder what else he took."

"This Sadie, whoever she is, was probably his accomplice," Mac said.

Brenda smiled. "According to the novel, Sadie engaged Bridgett in a conversation in the sunroom while Logan murdered her husband in the upstairs sitting room. Annette states that Bridgett didn't know Logan was there at all. Sadie pretended to be there to ask for a housekeeping job. After Thomas was killed, Bridgett and Sadie went upstairs where Logan grabbed Bridgett before she had time to realize what was going on. That is when she was killed."

Mac shook his head in wonderment. "I think we now

have enough questions for Annette Pickard. I'll have someone go to her house in Pennsylvania and give her a ride back up here. I want to know how she knows all of this, and I want to know if what she knows is the truth."

Brenda's mind raced with the discoveries spelled out in the novel. This was no fiction, she thought. That evening she picked up the newspaper to read blaring headlines about the apprehension and indictment of Logan Clark for the 1982 murders of Bridgett and Thomas Mackey. It was a whirlwind of information and Brenda was pleased to know that the mystery had finally been solved.

When Mac got home, they gave themselves some respite with a walk along the seaboard, contemplating how it had all turned out.

Mac told her that Annette willingly came back with the two officers and admitted the novel was a true story. She confessed she and her father were close over the years and that she always knew he wasn't violent and didn't have it in him to kill anyone. "He has been a thief, but he's no murderer," she said. "My mother is the Sadie in my book. She was in on all of it, helping Logan carry out the murders. My mother talks a lot when she is drunk."

Mac told Annette he would send word for her mother to be picked up. Annette Pickard finished her statements, and left. She had an unused plane ticket in her purse and now was the time to use it to get home. After all of Annette's secrecy, once the book was published it turned out she was unable to keep the truth hidden.

Brenda read something of interest on the second page of the next evening's newspaper. "Mattie Pickard, former wife of notorious felon Hal Pickard, was found dead of natural causes, slumped over her kitchen table."

Brenda was tempted to call Annette and offer her sympathy. Mattie Pickard's death must have occurred while she was in Sweetfern Harbor undergoing interrogation. She wondered how the daughter would take the news of her mother's sudden death. After knowing all she did, Brenda surmised she probably had little sentiment on the matter at all. In fact, Annette Pickard may be relieved to know the woman was gone. Or perhaps she would feel regret that her mother didn't have to pay for crimes she had committed before her death.

She told Mac the news. "I just got word of it too, Brenda. The police discovered her body when they went to her home to pick her up. It looks like the alcoholism finally won. They are saying she died of natural causes, but I suspect her liver was shot. The police chief there has promised to let us know the autopsy results when they get them."

"I don't know if I believe she died naturally, or if foul play entered into it. Annette was here, so we know she didn't harm Mattie. Hal is in prison. Logan is in a jail cell right here in Sweetfern Harbor. I guess that means none of the obvious suspects could have harmed her, right? I'm interested in hearing the autopsy report as soon as you get it."

Mac sighed. "Just when I thought things were coming to an end on this case, something like this happens. I sure hope she died a natural death."

"If she didn't, the problem will be handled in Scranton. That's one thing we won't have to deal with."

Mac knew Brenda had a good point. Still, he felt uneasy about the sudden death of a woman involved in a cold case in Sweetfern Harbor. "She would have been a good witness against Logan Clark. I planned to offer her a good deal so she would testify against him."

Brenda understood how Mac felt. She didn't like loose ends either, but there was nothing they could do about Mattie Pickard now. She searched for words and realized they had a sure way of getting a guilty verdict against Logan Clark.

"Logan confessed to the murders on tape. He even gave details. I'm surprised he didn't hold back on everything he knew."

"I think he confessed like that because he knew about the hard feelings Mattie held against him," Mac said. "He knew she would tell everything. And then the book came out and Logan probably guessed that Annette wrote the truth in it. His chances of proving innocence dwindled considerably." Mac paused. "We have fingerprints and DNA that proves he was involved." Mac sat up straight. "You don't think Logan had anything to do with Mattie's sudden death, do you?"

"I don't think he had time to make it to Pennsylvania and then manage to get into Canada in such a short time," Brenda protested. Mac agreed with his wife.

"I don't mean to change the subject so abruptly," Mac said, "but did you ever figure out how the key got separated from the metal chest? And how your uncle came to have it?"

"We may never know that," Brenda said, "but perhaps it was carelessly thrown away and Randolph simply found it." There were many things Brenda wished she could ask her uncle, and this was another mystery. She felt lucky it had helped them solve a cold case murder, even though so many questions were left hanging afterward.

Annette took the third exit and finally reached home again. Things were coming together and her father would be exonerated from all suspicion regarding the 1982 murders at last. It was too bad her mother wasn't alive to testify against her former lover, but knowing Mattie, Annette trusted only one thing about her mother—her fickle nature. One look at Logan could easily have rekindled her desperate hope for a future with him. All reason would have left Mattie as soon as she laid eyes on the man. The cops didn't have a reliable witness in her to begin with.

She unlocked her door and went inside. Everything was ready to finish packing up and she could be on her way. Her publisher told her that book sales were already going better than any of her other books. She hadn't told him the book was anything other than fiction. She had no intention of ever divulging that fact. Let everyone think she made it all up. The cops had to be allowed to carry through until Logan Clark was behind bars for the rest of his life. The lucrative royalties would be more than enough to allow her to live wherever she wanted.

Annette thought about her father. She would love to have him live with her once he got out of prison again, but she couldn't risk that. Knowing his nature, he would continue to live the life he knew so well. She couldn't tarnish her good name by being connected with him. No one understood that better than Hal Pickard. He loved his daughter and that was why he lived all these years keeping his distance from her.

Two days later, Annette left her home behind, fully furnished. The realtor she had contacted already had it listed. She arrived at the airport and found the gate where her plane would take off for Naples, Italy in three hours. She passed through security and sat alone to call her father. He expected the call and told her congratulations on her book. He had heard it was selling well. Neither mentioned the authenticity of her words; they didn't have to, nor was it safe to discuss it. She had a quick message for him, but before she delivered it, she told him she would call him once in a while to make sure he was fine.

"My number may be different, but I'll let you know if I do change it. I love you, Dad."

"I love you, too," he said. "Will 'Sadie' go with you?"

"I had to take Sadie to the veterinarian recently. As it turned out, she had a terminal illness and had to be put to sleep." Her father's shocked silence made her grin.

She ended the call before either of them tripped up. Her flight would leave soon, and she felt satisfied that finally, everything was going her way. It was a fitting end to the story and she couldn't have dreamed up a better one if she had written it herself.

more from wendy

about wendy meadows

Wendy Meadows is a USA Today bestselling author whose stories showcase women sleuths. To date, she has published dozens of books, which include her popular Sweetfern Harbor series, Sweet Peach Bakery series, and Alaska Cozy series, to name a few. She lives in the "Granite State" with her husband, two sons, two mini pigs and a lovable Labradoodle.

Join Wendy's newsletter to stay up-to-date with new releases. As a subscriber, you'll also get BLACKVINE MANOR, the complete series, for FREE!

Join Wendy's Newsletter Here
wendymeadows.com/cozy

Made in United States
North Haven, CT
13 April 2022

18207281R00065